TRAPPING FOG

A Slice of Steampunk

William Stafford

Trapping Fog
Published in 2016 by
Acorn Books
www.acornbooks.co.uk
an imprint of
Andrews UK Limited
www.andrewsuk.com

For Noel

TRAPPING FOG

One

I pounded my fists on the underside of the coffin lid. It did not budge. Neither did it make a hollow sound.

Crap, I thought. I'm buried alive.

Again!

I lay still and wondered how long I would have to wait this time, casting my mind back to the last thing I could remember before my death – before my 'supposed' death.

A hospital. Well, more of a dumping ground, really, for the sick and infirm of old London Town. The place had been packed, crammed to the rafters, with people in need – and the din! It was like Bedlam – which was across the road. The doctors couldn't cope. It was all they could do to provide enough space for the poor bastards to get horizontal. And they was all poor – of course they was. No one with any money would be seen dead in a place like that.

I reckoned it had been about mid-afternoon when I was pronounced (presumed!) dead. That meant another few hours until dusk and then a few more until midnight. Doctor Hoo would probably wait until then before he came to retrieve his employee.

Mind you, I don't know how long I've been out, I reflected. I'd taken the powder like he told me – I could still taste its vile bitterness – and let it work its magic. I can only assume Doctor Hoo had strode in, cloak swirling, and imperiously demanded the urgent removal of the corpse. Contamination, he would have said, along with a few other big words; the fellow must be interred with the utmost urgency.

And they, the overworked doctors and nurses, would have been impressed by his haughty manner, his implacable features, his

1

hundred-yard stare. More than anything they would be glad of one less poor bugger to think of, one less drop to worry about in this ocean of human misery.

The rozzers might even have heard about my demise by now… I couldn't help smiling, even in my coffin – There's not many people what can say that, is there? They can cross me off their list of wanted men. I am free!

Well, apart from the whole being-shut-up-in-a-coffin thing, but that was only a temporary inconvenience.

No, Damien, I warned myself. You take it easy. Doctor Hoo has come through for you yet again and all you have to do now is lie back, get some kip maybe, and try not to think of how full your bloody bladder is right now…

It was easy to doze off. The powder was still in my system. I could only hope I wouldn't piss myself while I slept.

Hurry up, Doctor Hoo! Get me out of here!

***

I woke to the sounds of scraping and the thud of a shovel blade against the other side of the lid. A few agonising moments later, there were creaks as the lid was prised off by a crowbar and then – oh, then! – cool air on my face and the smell of damp earth. Two hulking figures were standing over me, black shapes against the midnight sky. I squinted and shielded my eyes with my hand; they was shining their lantern right in front of my nose.

"Bloody hell!" cried one.

"We've got a live one!" added the other, no less shocked.

In their scramble to get out of the grave, the lantern was dropped. It burst into flames, licking hungrily at the men and leaping onto their overcoats. I sat up – the coffin was burning. Now, I've got nothing against cremation but this wasn't the time or the place so I sprang out and clambered over the flailing men and hauled myself out onto the ground. Every man for himself in these situations; you know how it is – or perhaps you don't. Perhaps your life is more normal than mine. I lay back on the mound of earth. At my feet, the grave blazed like a pit of Hell, the cries of the men the screams of the damned.

I drank in the fresh air like it was the first pint after a week of sobriety and couldn't help being startled to see a gaunt figure standing over me. Dressed in black, his opera cloak hanging to his ankles like the wings of a giant bat, and the sheen of his top hat catching the glimmer of the flames, Doctor Hoo raised his cane to his lips and blew twice in quick succession. Poisoned darts appeared in the necks of the burning men, silencing and toppling them instantly.

I got up. "Thanks, Doc." I wiped a hand on my shirt and offered it. As ever, he ignored it. "I knew you wouldn't let me down."

Doctor Hoo's face betrayed no emotion. From his cloak he produced a shovel. I accepted it; I knew what had to be done. I set to refilling the grave, dousing the fire and covering the men. Doctor Hoo did not linger – he's not one for physical labour; it's what he pays me for.

Satisfied I was on my Jack Jones, I unbuttoned my breeches and relieved myself at last. Ahh… Talk about making a pleasure of a necessity.

Steam rose from the grave.

No offence intended, I saluted the dead men and got back to shovelling.

Two

"There's been another one, sir." Sergeant Adams burst into Bow Street nick with his cheeks as livid as his ginger beard. Inspector John Kipper, whose facial hair was sparse and dull in comparison, peered over the top of his newspaper.

"There never has!" he exclaimed. "Another what, for Gawd's sake?"

"Another murder!" Adams was on the verge of stamping his foot. "Another dollymop down in Whitechapel, dressed up in her own insides like a blimmin' Christmas tree."

Kipper crumpled his broadsheet and got to his feet, reaching for his hat from the hook behind the door. "Who found her? Did you?"

"Lawks, no! Bobby on the beat stumbled across her. Well, stumbled into her, to be more precise. Poor chap. Been puking his ring up ever since. Only been on the job for a week and all. He's as white as a sheet what's seen a ghost."

"Yes, yes," Kipper waved impatiently. He strode along the corridor, expecting the sergeant to follow. "Enough about the boy. What about the girl?"

"The who, sir?"

"The victim! Who'd you think I meant? Princess Beatrice?"

"No, sir!" Adams quailed. "Don't bear thinking about, does it? If Foggy Jack got his mitts on a Royal or somebody important." He shuddered. Kipper came to a halt and glowered at him.

"Don't call him that!"

"Who?"

"Our killer."

"What? Foggy J—"

4

"Don't call him that!"

"It's what the papers is calling him on account of as how we can't catch him. He just melts away like the mist, leaving no clues behind."

Kipper growled. "I'll thank you not to repeat what the papers say, Sergeant. They'd sensationalise a bran tub at a church fete if they thought there was something in it for them."

Adams frowned. "In the tub, sir?"

Give me strength, Kipper sent up a silent prayer. "I mean, if it meant they'd sell more papers. That's the only thing they care about. Call me a hansom."

"You're handsome, sir. Like an oil painting of Prince Albert himself, Gawd rest him."

Adams held open the door to the street and saluted as Kipper went through it. "You're a funny bugger, Adams, and no mistake."

"Thank you, sir!" The ginger moustaches bristled with pride.

There was a cab waiting; Adams was more efficient than he appeared. Kipper was glad he didn't have to wait in the chill, evening air. Drops of moisture condensed on his hat and overcoat.

It's a foggy one, right enough, he thought as he climbed into the carriage.

"Whitechapel," he instructed the driver. He sat back, steeling himself for the scene ahead. You develop a strong stomach for things like this over the years but nothing could prepare you for the gory excesses of Foggy – he stopped himself – of this particular killer.

Perhaps the papers were right. Or perhaps they were understating the case. Perhaps you couldn't be sensational enough to depict the true horrors perpetrated by Foggy Jack.

Damn it, Kipper punched his own thigh. Got me doing it now.

***

It was not quite history repeating. It was more like current events stuck in a loop, Kipper reflected as he alighted from the cab. He dismissed the driver – there was no need to pay because the cab companies had an arrangement with the force. The Peelers were some of their best customers.

It was the same as the previous two occasions. Same kind of narrow alley. Same crowd of gawkers barely kept in check by a handful of bobbies. And beyond the cordon... Things would differ there somewhat, for the killer was imaginative, to say the least, in varying the presentations of his victims. He could get a job, Kipper mused, dressing windows for butchers and abattoirs.

"Sir," a constable nodded a greeting and lifted the rope. Kipper nodded back and ducked under. The ground squelched beneath the soles of his boots. There was nothing unusual in that, for you can find all manner of filth fouling London streets, but Kipper did not need to look down to confirm what his nose was telling him. He was stepping in – almost wading through – the victim's blood.

He pressed a handkerchief to his nose and mouth and pressed on. The walls of the narrow alley sloped ever closer together and at the point where there was only a couple of feet between them, there she was. Hanging several feet off the ground like washing on a line.

Blood continued to trickle from the gaping hole in her abdomen, running down her legs and dripping from the heels of her shoes, adding to the pool on the cobbles below. Adams's bobby had been right; she did look something akin to a Christmas tree. Her guts had been yanked from her body and draped around her like festive trimmings.

Christmas lights, Kipper mused grimly.

He addressed the bobby who was guarding the scene with his eyes studiously averted.

"Get her down," he ordered curtly, glad that the task was not his. Things would get gruesome enough in Kipper's near future come the autopsy.

He returned to the street, trying to ignore the slaps and splashes his feet made and beckoned to a second constable. "Go back there and help him," he nodded over his shoulder. Then he addressed the crowd. There was more than a few painted faces jockeying for position and straining to see. "We need to find out who she is. If any of you have any idea, report to Bow Street with some urgency. We need to get this bastard off the streets. For all our sakes."

"Here!" squawked a woman with peroxided hair. "Wha's the reward?"

"Yeah!" grunted a few of the others.

Kipper responded with a scowl. "Your reward will be me turning a blind eye to your business. Your reward will be, when I've caught him, to go about that business in safety. It's in your interests to speak out. Any shred, any scrap of information might lead to the bastard what done this swinging from a rope. Surely that's worth a few minutes of your precious time."

A police wagon arrived. The breath of the horses plumed in the evening air, making chimneys of their nostrils. Two men, their faces masked with scarves against the stench, carried a stretcher into the alley. Kipper climbed up to sit with the driver while the men carried out their grisly task.

The crowd gasped as the body was brought out, covered in blankets. One of the men's feet slipped in the spilled blood, jolting the stretcher and causing an arm as pale and lifeless as any rag doll's to drop over the edge. The women screamed. A couple of them fainted.

Kipper rode back to the nick. A clock struck eleven. Good job I've got no home life to speak of, he thought.

Three

Doctor Hoo let me recover at his gaff in Limehouse. I had to fill my own bath, mind; he's not one for running around after others. He didn't even tell me where the kettle was, and do you know, I've never seen him so much as sip a cup of tea, and I thought they was famous for it. Tea. Orientals. I thought it was even more sacred to them than the great British cuppa is to the English. But what do I know? Sweet Fanny Whojimmyflop, that's what.

Well, I had me a good old rummage in the little kitchen. The place looked like it hadn't been touched for donkeys' and I had to evict a big fat hairy spider from the copper before I could fill it, having to coax water from the rusted pump in the yard – well, it was dust at first and then came sludge. My arm was sore before I got to anything resembling Adam's Ale.

Adams! *That* was Sweet Fanny's name. I know that much at least.

Well, I was more exhausted than ever by the time I'd boiled that kettle half a dozen times and I reckon I must have stunk to high heaven, on account of how much I was sweating and what with the reek of that grave still on me. I've never been so happy to have a bath in all my born days, I can tell you.

I splashed about a bit, giving all me nooks and crannies and dangly bits a good wash – especially the dangly bits – and then I lay back for a good old soak. I almost dropped orf, it was so relaxing, but then I heard voices – or rather, one voice, dominating the discussion, because he don't say much, don't Doctor Hoo, and when he does it's always very quiet.

So I sits up. I've cleaned the dirt from my earholes and I can hear their conversation like I was in the same room with them. Which

I just about was, on account of the little kitchen space was only a corner of the old warehouse, partitioned off by wooden walls. The top half of these walls was all panes of glass, and me, being low in the tub, they (Hoo and his loudmouth chum) couldn't see me, but I could hear them all right.

"It's not good enough," the loudmouth kept saying. He sounded like he'd got a right strop on – and posh! It sounded to me like he was not only hoity but toity and all, with a receding chin and a nose made out of toffee and all, I shouldn't wonder. He was giving Doctor Hoo a right ear-bashing, like he was a servant or something what had traipsed horses' apples onto his best Persian carpet. I'd never heard no one speak to Doctor Hoo like that and I could imagine his face, like a mask carved out of stone, not moving. And his eyes, like black beads of glass, just staring, patient, like that spider I'd made homeless, waiting to pounce. And his thin moustaches, hanging down past his chin like untied shoelaces. And his skin the colour of old paper – but here's me rattling on about what Hoo looks like when I should be telling you what the posh git was banging on about because it's more relevant and pertinent and all the rest of it.

"It's not good enough, dash it!" he hit something – probably punching the palm of his other hand. The floorboards creaked as he stamped around. He was getting himself worked up into a right old how's-your-father. "What am I paying you for, man? And don't give me that rot about awaiting a shipment from the East; it has been six months already. I know what you types are like. Probably squandering my money in some opium den, I wouldn't be surprised. I want results, man. I'm not getting any younger. Quite the contrary, in fact, and this leg is driving me to distraction."

Oh yeah, I thought? It don't seem to be stopping you marching around like you own the place. Which he probably did. Or he was paying the rent or something like that.

My interest was piqued, you might say. I didn't even notice me water going cold. At one time, I didn't know nothing about Hoo's business. I thought he was a doctor, like in doctor. You know, the sort what gives you a powder and a hefty bill to go with it. Turned out he weren't. Well, not just. You know, you can be a doctor of anything. It don't have to be medicine. Oh no, you can even be a doctor of music. How does that work? Here, doc, can you come around and fix the leg on my piano? I don't understand this world we live in.

I don't know what kind of doctor Doctor Hoo was exactly but it certainly wasn't pianos.

"It's my twenty-fifth birthday next month," the posh git was whining now. Pleading. "Do you think you will be able to do anything for me before then? If it's a question of funding…"

I heard the unmistakable sound of money being slapped on a table. Things had just got more interesting.

"Tomorrow," said Doctor Hoo, almost too quiet but I heard it. "Return at midnight."

The posh git, his anger all run out, was all thank-yous and bless-yous. He'd let off his steam and Hoo hadn't risen to it. It's like arguing with a post; you can't keep it up for long, you get nothing back.

"Until tomorrow, then," the posh git said. I waited until I heard the door close again before I stuck my head out.

Doctor Hoo was standing by the table. He was like that post I mentioned only someone had dressed it in a cloak and topper and carved a face into it, like a totem pole.

"Aye, aye!" I clicked my tongue and nodded at the cash. "You've got your chink, then."

The face didn't move but the eyes seemed to bore into me. Had I said the wrong thing? I was going to explain that where I come from 'chink' means money. Cold hard cash. The sound it makes as you jiggle it in your pocket. But Doctor Hoo turned his face away ever so slowly and ever so slightly. I followed where his eyes went.

In the corner was a large trunk, bursting with clothes. I scurried across to it, one hand on my privates and the other on my bum, although he wasn't even looking; I'd put money on it.

The clothes was all men's clothes, all different sizes. I pulled out a shirt and a pair of trousers and gave them a sniff. They didn't smell too mildewed or nothing so I put them on. Perhaps he was a doctor of clobber and all! A professor of menswear.

Hoo pointed a long, skeletal finger, encased in a glove of black leather, at a straw pallet in a corner, indicating that I might spend the night there if I wanted. The hour was late and I didn't fancy the hike back to my Whitechapel stamping ground so I took him up on the offer.

"Talk about your lap of luxury." I tested the mattress. Three species of beetle and an earwig darted for cover. Charming. Doctor Hoo stalked off to some other part of the warehouse, where his own billet was situated, I shouldn't wonder, leaving me in darkness like the light had gone out of my life.

I couldn't sleep. Well, I'd had some shut-eye earlier on, you'll recall, when I was banged up in that coffin and besides, that wooden crate, fashioned though it was for a pauper's burial, was a damn sight more comfortable than that colony of wayward invertebrates, my straw pallet. I could hear them moving about under my head. I could imagine them creeping and crawling all over me and eating me alive with their little cake holes. Every inch of my skin tingled. Every hair on my body stood on its end. One thing was clear: there would be no rest for Damien Deacus that night.

There was something else and all. A faint tap-tapping in the distance, like a self-conscious woodpecker. Once I'd heard it, I couldn't not hear it, and what with me six-legged bedfellows, it was enough to drive me both up the wall and round the bleedin' twist, so I got up, shook and patted myself, jumped up and down to dislodge any stowaways, and went in search of the source of that blasted tap-tap-tapping.

It's a good job that warehouse was mostly empty but you can bet your old granny if there's something in the dark, my trusty shinbone will find it. I'm telling you, the coppers should employ me to find missing persons or stolen goods or something. As long as they're in the dark, I'll find them.

Sure enough, bang, crash, wallop! I collided with something solid and was forced to let out a bit of a swear. I hopped around, rubbing my offended bone and trying to keep the noise to a minimum. The last thing I wanted was old Hoo to come back and chuck me out for kicking up such a palaver. I fished in me trouser pockets for a handkerchief or something with which to stem the flow of curses by stuffing it in my gob – only to remember that they wasn't my trousers. I'd had them out of that trunk where there was so many pairs to choose from… Well, the pockets was empty but I was given cause to wonder all over again where Hoo had got them all from and what for. None of them was the kind of thing he'd be seen dead in and he didn't seem the type to organise a jumble sale out of the goodness of his heart.

A familiar whiff teased my old hooter. The smell of dirt and damp and musty cellars. It ain't me, I thought with confidence, because I'd just had me a bath. Something in the back of my head clicked: them clothes must have been where I'd been. Them clothes must have been dug up like what I was.

I felt disgusted. Having dead men's clothes on me. I think that was getting my goat more than the fact that they'd been robbed from somebody's coffin.

Think, Damien, think! Nobody goes to the trouble of breaking the law against digging people up just because they want new togs. It's the bodies they're after. Now, you hear all sorts of tales of doctors paying felons to fetch them freshly buried bodies so they can dismantle them and learn all sorts about human anatomy and bits and pieces what you can't get from a book.

Putting aside my cringes and woes about wearing some bloke's funeral suit, I stole across the warehouse floor to a metal staircase that spiralled up to an upper storey kind of thing. Mezzanine – that's the word. Or am I thinking about Italian grub?

Clang!

My trusty shinbone found the lowermost step with ease. Bugger me! Limping, I climbed the stairs to investigate. The tap-tap-tapping was a little bit louder now and was coming from behind a door, through the opaque glass of which was shining the dim light of an oil lamp.

Something was afoot…

I twisted the knob ever so slightly and, giving the door a gentle push, I went inside.

With his back to the door, Doctor Hoo was working at a bench; I don't think he heard me come in but I froze just in case, and tried to see what he was up to.

The tap-tapping stopped and he reached for something from a wooden box to his left, rummaging through it before his fingers – still gloved – closed on what he wanted. I found myself drifting closer – There is something about somebody absorbed in his work that draws you in. From my new vantage point, I could see what was on the bench, illuminated by a pool of light spilling from the oil lamp.

Cogs. Springs. Dials.

All the time I've known him, he's always tinkering with something. To look at him, you wouldn't peg dear old Doctor Hoo as a clock doctor! A clocktor, you might say. Well, you probably wouldn't call him 'dear' neither.

"That tool," he said without turning around. Somehow or other he'd clocked me! My bloody shinbone must have given him the head's up.

"This one?" I picked up a spindly screwdriver. He nodded and took it from me. He used it to tighten something so teeny

I couldn't see it. It was only then that I noticed he was wearing huge spectacles with lenses like the bottoms of jam jars. His eyes loomed large behind them – it was quite startling.

"Here," I said. "Moonlighting, are you, as a whatdyoucallit, a doctor of clockery?"

"Horologist," he said without looking from his task.

"Really? I would have thought they was all about dollymops."

He ignored me and continued to make adjustments to the curved contraption that was gripped in a vice. It was made of brass, for the most part, five overlapping crescents behind which the workings formed an intricate maze of gears and little wheels. I'm no whore expert but I could tell it weren't no timepiece. It was a thing of beauty though, I have to say, whatever it was.

Hoo turned to me and fixed me with his magnified stare. "You are loyal," he said slowly and I couldn't tell if it was a question or a staff appraisal.

"O' course," I said. "I ain't going to turn in the geezer what saved my life now, am I?"

His eye twitched at 'geezer' – I wouldn't have spotted it if it weren't for them spectacles.

"You are honourable, then," he nodded.

"You know me: honour among thieves and all that."

Another twitch, slightly bigger. I think he preferred it when I was calling him a geezer.

"Wait," he instructed. He moved away from the bench, taking the oil lamp with him. "Do not touch," he added as an afterthought and I rammed my hands into me pockets before they could pilfer any of them shiny brass doings. And then I rammed them out again – if such a thing is possible – remembering they was dead man's pockets. So I took to whistling, as you do when you want to come across as all innocent and that.

All of a sudden he was back and I never heard a thing. With the oil lamp on top, he was carrying a crate of the sort you see in Billingsgate what had fish in it. Dead ones, I mean. Well, they wouldn't last long in there because all the water would leak out. Anyway, he hadn't brought me a spot of fish supper. He put the oil lamp on the bench and then lifted the lid off the crate and it took him no effort at all even though it was plain to see it was nailed down. It would have taken me a jemmy or a hammer and chisel at least. He's deceptively strong, is Doctor Hoo.

The crate was packed with ice so I thought perhaps we was in for a bit of fresh fish after all. I could murder fish and chips right about now, I reckoned, and my stomach gurgled and leapt like a puppy begging at the dinner table.

Hoo delved his hands into the ice. His leather gloves protected him from the cold and he pulled out something long and pink like a joint of meat. So, it weren't fish on the menu, it was pork. He placed the joint on the bench top and tilted the lamp so we could get a better squint at it. And I saw it was a joint all right but not a joint of pork. It was a human joint, a blimmin' leg from the knee down to the toes. I told you something was a foot! Doctor Hoo rolled it over, peering at it through those magnifying spectacles. His face never gives much away but I could tell he was pleased with it. I backed away. No, thank you. Not even with chips.

Where would he get his hands on a bloke's leg?

Well, it might seem obvious to you but it took a while to dawn on me. It was as though I'd forgotten where I'd just been.

Grave-robbing.

Of course!

Not that Doctor Hoo would get his own brass bands dirty, oh no! He paid blokes, like them two bruisers what catched fire and got buried to do all the dirty work.

Hoo picked up the contraption he'd been working on and proceeded to attach it to the top of the leg like a cap for the knee. A kneecap cap, I suppose. He stood the foot on the table and then

15

twiddled something on the device. The foot kicked out sharply, knocking the lamp over and plunging us into darkness.

A chill ran down my backbone as I heard a sound unlike any other, a sound I'd never heard before.

Doctor Hoo was laughing.

Four

Inspector Kipper rubbed his eyes and looked at the clock. It was almost three a.m. I'll forget where my home is, he thought sourly. He perused the information on his desk one last time, the words swimming on the pages in front of him, making no sense. Too tired. Perhaps he should go home and get a few hours' kip.

The nick was quiet. Even the drunkards in the cells were asleep, snoring like contented kittens. There was the duty sergeant reading *The Strand* on the front desk but apart from that, Kipper was alone in the building. Anyone with an ounce of sense had gone to their beds hours ago.

He stood on weary feet and reached for his coat and muffler. Home seemed like a long way away. Well, it's not really home, he reflected. Just a place to go. He sat down again and riffled through the papers on his desk one more time.

Her name had been Miggles. Amelia Miggles, known as Millie. She was nineteen from somewhere in the West Country – those who had come forth to speak to the police were unable to say where exactly. Like most of the dollymops, Millie had no known next of kin.

Poor girl. What brought you to London, eh? The old streets-are-paved-with-gold bollocks? The promise of fame and fortune? Or what drove you from home? That was another way to look at it. What did you run away from? And could it have been any worse than the way things turned out for you? Kipper could think of nothing worse than what happened to Millie Miggles, winding up as the third victim of a maniac. Not quite the fame you'd perhaps been seeking, eh?

He scanned the preliminary hand-written report from the morgue. Evisceration was given as the cause of death. Dressing it up in big words didn't make it any more palatable. A sharp knife, perhaps of the kind used by butchers, was proposed as the murder weapon. Or a scalpel, a surgical scalpel. Either way, the killer knew what he was doing. The wounds were not haphazard, born of homicidal frenzy. They were precisely where they needed to be in order to achieve the desired effect.

Kipper scribbled two notes on a pad.

Smithfield

Harley Street

Both seemed good places to start and, with the dawn only a couple of hours away, the meat market would be awash with butchers. The enquiries could begin along with the new day.

Kipper's eyelids drooped. His head bobbed and jerked on his neck. Before he knew it was happening, he was drifting off—

—along a dark alleyway of cobbles and puddles, where the fog from the street didn't quite penetrate. A woman on a corner cackled 'Hello, dearie' sizing him up with wary eyes. He hurried along, turning corner after corner – the alley seemed inordinately long. At every corner another woman. Or perhaps the same woman, the same corner, making the same offer: 'Chuck your muck, sir?' and giving him the same languid appraisal. He stopped; he had an idea of asking one of the women the way out, the way back to the street, the way home. He would pay for the answer. He fished a guinea from his pocket to show willing but the coin came out dripping with blood and the woman's mouth broadened into a grin, and the grin kept on gaping wider until it split her face and the blood poured out and the fog swirled around and Kipper could no longer see and he—

"Morning, sir!" Sergeant Adams was standing over him with a cup and saucer. "Nice drop of Rosie Lee."

Kipper composed himself and cleared his throat, grunting his thanks.

Adams was perusing the papers, twisting his neck to try to read them better. "Nasty business and no mistake," he concluded. Kipper shuffled the papers together and put them in a wallet. "There's a cab waiting, sir. I'll tell him five minutes."

"Thank you." Kipper nodded at the cup of tea. Adams put it on the desk. Kipper waited until the sergeant had gone before he picked it up. He didn't want Adams to see how much his hands were shaking.

***

The dawn only served to cast a dim glow on the fog. The cab picked its way slowly through the streets, the horse as tentative as though it was crossing thin ice. In the carriage, Kipper was waxing impatient. He had a headache from lack of sleep and his neck and back were protesting every jolt and bounce.

Smithfield, formerly 'Smooth field' had once been an outdoor market and could trace its heritage back to medieval times. Kipper wondered what wares they would have hawked back then. Dragon meat probably. And hawks.

In more recent times, great halls had been erected so at least indoors and out of the fog, you had a good chance of getting a proper look at what you were buying even if it was no help identifying what your purchase might be. Kipper knew, when times were hard (and when were they anything else?) unscrupulous merchants would pass off cat meat as rabbit or lamb.

There were still some external stalls with red and white awnings, showing in the fog like bloodstains. And, even at first light, the place was bustling with trade. As early as two a.m. buyers would flock in to secure fresh supplies for the city's shops and hotels. It's a glimpse into another world, thought Kipper. An underworld that is, for the most part, legit. And, of course, if the killer is a butcher, it would be easy to filter out those who had alibis by checking with market officials who had opened up their stalls when and on which nights…

He entered the first hall he came to, a grey monument of dilapidated grandeur, and pulled his muffler down. As well as the din of commerce, the stench of the place assaulted him like a mugger. The stink evoked the scene of Millie Miggles's slaughter.

Blood is blood; animal or human, the stink of it is the same. Kipper coughed and lifted his scarf again but then, realising it might appear as though he had come to rob the place, steeled himself and uncovered his mouth again.

"Now then, sir," a burly, jovial fellow with forearms like ham hocks and a complexion as ruddy as the stains on his apron. "What can I do you for? Got a lovely batch of tripe right here."

Kipper flashed his warrant card. "I don't want tripe," he said. "I want answers."

The butcher's smile faltered but he continued to prepare cuts for his display. With a long-bladed filleting knife, Kipper noted. But then a cursory glance at surrounding stalls revealed that no butcher worth his salted pork would be without such an implement.

"If it's about them suckling pigs, I bought them in good faith, so I did."

"No—"

"How was I to know they was mutts? They come to me with their skins off. Heads, feet, the lot off."

"Surely a man with your experience can tell pork from mutton."

"No, mate, not mutton. Mutts. Bow-wows. Doggies."

"Oh…" Kipper considered this for a moment and forced himself back to the matter in hand. "It's not about the bow-wows. Do you come here every night?"

The butcher smirked. "Are you giving me the glad eye, Inspector? Because I ain't into that but I've heard tell of a molly house not far from here."

Kipper reddened. The butcher chuckled and dealt with a particularly obstinate piece of gristle.

"Every night – except Saturday night, Sunday morning. Market's shut of a Sunday morning, praise the Lord."

"You're a religious man?" To Kipper it seemed unlikely – unless the religion involved grisly sacrifices.

"Nah, mate, but a man needs a lie-in. The body needs rest. You look fit for the knacker's yard yourself, if you don't mind me saying."

That's true enough, thought Kipper. He sorted through his notes. None of the murders had been committed on a Saturday night or Sunday morning. So this fellow at least was off the butcher's hook.

"Anything else I can help you with, only I've got customers?"

Kipper became aware of men queuing behind him, sporting the livery of London's swankiest hotels. He thanked the butcher for his time, tipped his hat and moved on, almost getting trampled by a dozen or so cows being led through the hall. Docile creatures, Kipper observed; dewy-eyed and wet-nosed, they trudged by, little suspecting what fate lay in store for them, not knowing that bits and pieces of their kind were hanging from hooks all around.

"Mind out!" laughed the toothless cowherd. "Or you'll be taken in with them. Get your bonce bashed in before you know it!"

Highly amused with himself, the cowherd swatted at a rump with a switch. It took Kipper a few seconds to realise he had been insulted.

"Can I help you, mate?"

Kipper spun around to find a man in a greasy bowler hat and even greasier overall peering at him. Kipper showed his warrant card and the fellow's demeanour changed at once.

"Listen," he broke out in a sweat, "I didn't know they was swans. I thought they was big quails. Really big quails."

"That's not why I'm here," said Kipper. "But I do need to see your records. Who books which stall and when. You must have such a thing?"

The fellow straightened with a look of injured pride. "Of course! In the old days, it was first come, first pick. Folks would set up their pitch anywhere they liked. It was chaos."

Kipper glanced around at the melee and the clamour and was unable to imagine a scene of greater disorder. "I'd be obliged if you'd show me, Mr – ah?"

"Ratcliff," the man nodded. "Irving Ratcliff, general supervisor. My office is this way."

He led the inspector through the market hall where the high ceiling amplified the din of the transactions under way as well as the sound of the cleavers hacking through bone and into wooden blocks. An eerie scream pierced the air.

"What was that?" Kipper froze.

"Cattle," shrugged the general supervisor. "They knows they're in for it. They can smell the fear and the blood or something. Don't worry, they soon shuts up when the hammer smashes their skulls in."

Kipper was less than reassured.

"Of course, I thought for a minute you was here with yet another bleedin' complaint. We get them all the time."

"Complaints?"

"The noise, the smell, the animals. Oh, it's cruel, people say. Oh, it don't half pong! Hypocrisy, says I. They just don't like it on their doorstep. They wants it on their plates and served up in aspic or a fancy French sauce but they don't want to know where it comes from. It ain't a pretty picture – nobody's saying it is. But if you want meat for dinner you have to accept a bit of murder in your life. I mean, it don't grow on trees, does it? Here, are you all right, Inspector? Only you've gone a bit green around the gills."

Kipper offered a weak smile. He ran a finger under his collar in a bid to loosen it a little and then dabbed at his brow with his handkerchief. "I'm fine," he lied.

"Through here." Ratcliff opened a door and ushered the inspector in. Closing the door muffled the din and stifled the stench – for which Kipper was grateful.

The room was home to a table and chair and stack upon stack of papers and ledgers. Nevertheless, Ratcliff was able to lay his hands on what he wanted without a moment's delay.

"Here you go. Market diary going back five years or more. Who had what pitch and when and who still hasn't bleedin' paid for it."

He slammed a pile of thick tomes, each of them bulging like overstuffed upholstery, on the already cluttered table top. Kipper was daunted by the amount of paperwork before him and he'd thought coppers had it bad.

He took out his notebook. "There's three dates I'm interested in. Any of your regulars fail to show up on these nights? Or did any leave early? Turn up late?"

Ratcliff glanced at the list and frowned. "What's all this in aid of, Inspector? I am allowed to arsk, ain't I? On account of me being so cooperative and all."

Kipper was tight-lipped. "I'm just following a hunch."

"That's funny," said Ratcliff. "Most people's hunches follow them." He laughed. Kipper didn't. Something occurred to the market supervisor. "Here! It's about them murders, ain't it? All over the papers. Foggy Jack! You think one of my butchers is Foggy Jack!"

"I am not at liberty to—"

"You do! Well, I never! Here, I hope there's a reward in it if I helps you catch him."

"Well, I—"

"Only joking. Happy to help get that bastard off the streets. Give's them dates again."

He reached for the notebook but commotion from outside caused him to swear and, shoving Kipper aside, burst from the office. Kipper followed but hung back in the doorway, clinging to a jamb for support. His legs were limp as sausage links and his face had taken on the pallor of beef dripping.

The market hall was in a state of clamour and confusion. A brown cow was careering between stalls, crashing into them more often than not. People were either chasing after the animal or trying to get out of its unpredictable path. The creature was stumbling and lurching at full pelt.

"Oh, bloody hell," Ratcliff complained, reaching for an axe from a wall. "Another one's got loose. Best keep out of its way."

The cow was bearing down on them, eyes rolling wildly, blood streaming down its snout from the wound in its skull. Kipper gasped to see the handle of a hammer protruding from that wound.

"This won't take a minute," Ratcliff glanced over his shoulder. He spun around, swinging the axe up, around and down into the animal's neck, but the cow kept coming, mewling in terror. Ratcliff struck again and again, severing a front leg at the knee. The cow toppled and at once a swarm of butchers was upon it, hacking and stabbing long after the beast was well and truly stilled.

"Phew," said Ratcliff, wiping a hand across his face and bloodying his forehead. "We could do without this sort of carry-on."

"Carrion," murmured Kipper, sliding down the doorpost in a swoon.

Five

Doctor Hoo gave me a white coat to put on and a surgical mask to cover my nose and mouth. We looked the same. Well, what I mean is we was dressed alike in our white coats and masks and little cotton caps. Only he was taller, wasn't he, Doctor Hoo. Well over six foot if he's an inch. Nearer seven, I shouldn't be surprised. He must have to go to a special tailor.

There was a knocking at the door but before I could scoot off to answer it, Doctor Hoo stuck his finger in the air (he was still wearing them gloves) to stop me.

"I'll do talking," he said. The mask over his mouth didn't budge. Throwing his voice, I'd wager, like one of the fellows I saw down the old music hall. Ventriloquist.

And guess who's the dummy.

Not me.

The dummy was on the other side of the warehouse door, knocking on it fit to bash it in. Doctor Hoo tilted his head, ever so slightly, and then I did scoot off to answer it.

It was a youngish chap. Early twenties, I reckon, with blond curls and piercing, although slightly bloodshot, blue eyes. His clobber was all posh and he had a silver-topped cane with which he had tried to bash the door down. Young then and not unhandsome but already his jawline was softened by a fondness for drink. One of your idle rich, then, what's never done an honest day's work in all his born days. All right, come to think of it, neither have I and I'm bleedin' skint so something's gone wrong somewhere.

"You there!" he barked and when he did I recognised the voice. It was him, weren't it? The toff that was stamping around and giving old Hoo an ear-bashing. "I am Edward," he said but it cut no ice with me. "Lord Beighton," he added, like that made it any nicer to meet him. "I say, is the doctor in?"

I bowed low and beckoned him in with a sweeping gesture – all sarcastic, mind, because I don't bow to nobody. In he stepped, unclasped his cloak and dropped it on top of me. The brass neck of it! He strode across the floor, limping a bit and twirling his cane. I bundled up the cloak – lovely bit of shmutter – and chucked it into a corner. Well. That's what you get when you don't tip the help.

He waited at the foot of the winding staircase. I don't know what for. Perhaps he was expecting me to give him a bleedin' piggyback or something! Remembering my instructions, I didn't make a peep. I bowed again and made gestures to him as if to say, Feel free to go up, my lord. In fact, we'd be honoured if you'd oblige.

Oh, I should have been on the stage because he copped my meaning right away and climbed the stairs, and it was all I could do not to laugh. Glad of that cotton mask I was and no mistake.

It was a bit of a struggle for him, climbing them stairs. He was puffing and panting and perspiring in no time. I waited until he got to the mezzanine at the top before I went up after – I didn't want him keeling over and tumbling down on top of me like we was bleedin' Jack and bleedin' Jill.

He was waiting outside the door and getting his breath back and he shot me an impatient look like it was me what had took my time and not him. I pointed at the floor as if to say, Wait here, and I went through the door to where Hoo was standing by his workbench, which was all cleared off and covered with a bright, white bedsheet. Hoo must have connexions with the local laundry, I shouldn't be surprised.

I jerked my thumb at the door behind me. "He's here," I whispered. Hoo stiffened; I'd broken his No Talking rule.

"Sorry," I said. His narrow eyes narrowed further. He nodded: I was to show our visitor in. With more bowing and arm-sweeping,

I shepherded the toff into the laboratory – 'cause that's what it was. Let's call a spade a bleedin' spade.

"Good day to you, Doctor," the toff said, leaning on his cane. He was sweating like a pig with a guilty conscience and his face was the colour of turned milk. He didn't look at all well. "Is it here? Is it ready?"

Hoo inclined his head in one of them slow, graceful nods of which he is a master. The answer perked the toff up considerably, almost to the point of clapping his hands.

"Then it shall be done today?" his eyes lit up with hope.

Hoo nodded again. "Now," he intoned, gesturing at how ready his table was and everything. He turned to me. "Gentleman's trousers," he said, baffling me at first. I frowned and I almost said, What about 'em? But then I cottoned on. He wanted me to take 'em off so I went to the toff and made for his belt. Well, he didn't like that and slapped my hands away.

"I can do it!" he snapped. "One learns how to survive on the butler's day orf."

He divested himself of his shoes and his trousers and handed them to me. I put them on a chair but I wasn't really paying attention. I couldn't stop staring. It was his leg. All green it was from the knee down to the ankle. Green and black and purple and oozing in places. Disgusting it was. Fair turned my stomach, it did. But I couldn't stop gawping at it like it was a freak show at the fair. He caught me looking and shooed me with his cane.

"Gangrene," he said.

I can see it has gone green, mate, I felt like saying. He hobbled over to the table and I had to help him climb on. He lay on the sheet and propped himself on his elbows, looking down the length of his horrible limb. "This is it, old stick," he said with a tremor of trepidation and a smidgeon of sentimentality in his voice. "Goodbye and all that. Thank you for all the support."

Blimey! I reckon if he could have reached it, he would have kissed his foot goodbye. I shouldn't mock though; I'm quite attached to my body parts and all.

Doctor Hoo held a folded hanky over the neck of a little brown bottle and upended it. Then he pressed the cloth over the toff's north and south and snuffed him out like a candle.

"Anaesthesia," said Hoo.

"Bless you," I replied.

What happened next was horrible. One of the worst things I ever had the misfortune to witness (up to that point). I'll spare you most of the details but after he'd tied a length of rubber tube around the toff's thigh, Hoo got involved in a lot of slicing and sawing. It's hard work, taking a man's leg off, but Hoo looked like he knew what he was doing and I couldn't help wondering how many times he'd done such a thing before. His eyes burned with concentration but he didn't break a sweat despite the physical effort.

Then it was off. Oh, it did whiff, that rotten old leg! Even through my mask. I backed away in case Hoo tried to pass it to me. I didn't want to touch it, not even with me gloves on. Hoo nodded to me to bring the wooden crate. It had been topped up with fresh ice, I noticed, to keep the toff's new leg fresh as a bleedin' daisy. The old leg was tossed unceremoniously into the crate.

Out came that brass contraption, the kneecap cap. Hoo attached it first to the stump – which took bleedin' ages because of threading the veins and arteries and whatsits through it. The cap was a link between the two bits of leg, you see. Hoo was wearing his magnifying specs and kept beckoning me to hold the lamp so he could get a better squint at what he was doing.

At long last, after an hour or two or three or four, it was done. Hoo stood up straight and allowed himself a sigh of satisfaction with a job well done.

"What's next?" I had to ask.

"You tidy up. Him sleep." He stalked out of the laboratory, leaving the toff snoring and oblivious and me wondering what the bleedin' hell I was going to do with that rotten old leg.

***

Well, I bundled up the bloodied sheets and stuffed them in a sack – perhaps Hoo's mates down the laundry would be able to do something with them stubborn stains, and good luck to 'em. I wasn't going to try. I'll do a lot of things for Doctor Hoo but I ain't no washerwoman.

I ran his tools under the pump and was careful to dry them, although I don't think they was made of stuff that rusts. Then, with one last look at Sleeping Beauty (well, Sleeping Long John Silver, more like!) I went downstairs to find Hoo standing slumped. Almost bent in half he was. He looked like a puppet hanging up after the show was over.

"Doctor..." I approached with caution in case all it was was he had fallen asleep standing up. I've heard of such a thing is possible but I'd never seen it before. His eyes was open but then I've heard about that and all, but his lips were set tight and it seemed to me he was struggling to right himself, like a beetle on its back. "Doctor? What is it? What's the matter?"

"Pocket..." he said, almost too quietly for my lugholes to pick up. "Left pocket..." His eyes rolled sideways in case I didn't bleedin' know my left from my right.

I put my hand in. Deep, them pockets are, on lab coats, and at first I couldn't find nothing but then my fingers closed on a scrap of paper. I pulled it out and squinted at it.

"This?"

All it was was a list of numbers. I read them out loud. Hoo tried to shake his head. He seemed to be getting slower and slower.

"Safe..." he uttered and his head dropped.

Oh, yeah, of course! The numbers was the combination for a safe. I won't write them down because Hoo swore me to secrecy. He didn't want the numbers falling into the wrong brass bands.

The safe was in the little kitchen bit, covered by an oilcloth. I'd been using it as a table. I cleared the tea things off of it and whipped the cloth away. I crouched and turned the dial this way and that, according to the numbers. Something clunked inside the door. I twisted the handle and lo and behold—

—Nothing!

I put my hand in and patted around until I found something right at the back of the shelf. I pulled it out. It was a key, one of that sort with a butterfly bow at the top and a hollow shaft with a square hole at the bottom. Like the kind you'd have to wind up a music box only bigger.

I hurried back with it to the doctor who was like a broken scarecrow by now, his legs buckling, one more than the other.

"This, Doctor?" I held the key under his nose. "Is this what you want?"

His gloved hand shot up and snatched the key from my palm, giving me quite a start.

"Go!" he urged. "Get out. Leave… me…"

I dillied and dallied, dallied and dillied.

"Go!" he barked like a rusty hinge. I bolted, back up them stairs to where the toff was sleeping it off. What the bleedin' hell was going on? I slumped against the back of the door.

Crikey, Damien Deacus, you don't half get mixed up with some rum sorts and no mistake.

Six

Inspector Kipper woke with a start. He blinked and rubbed his eyes, surprised to find himself back in his office at Bow Street nick. Sergeant Adams was in front of him, cup of tea at the ready.

"What?" Kipper looked at his surroundings with a dazed expression. "How did I—"

"Meat wagon brung you here, sir. You had quite a turn."

Kipper frowned. "Meat wagon? Do you mean the ambulance?"

"No, sir. The meat wagon. From the market. Dead to the world you was." Adams placed the cup and saucer on the desk like a votive offering. "You needs looking after, sir, if you don't mind my saying."

Kipper ignored that remark. He composed himself and sat up straight. Adams's eyes flickered to his notebook.

"A Mister Ratcliff, sir, sends you the ledgers you're interested in and his sincere good wishes for your swift recovery."

"Does he, indeed?" Kipper stirred the tea.

"Indeed he does, sir," Adams indicated a stack of ledgers on a chair. "Lot of paper there, I should say."

"You'd be right to," Kipper sipped.

"I'll get the men to start sifting through it right away, sir. Many hands and all that."

"What? Oh, yes!" It hadn't occurred to Kipper that he could delegate some of the drudgery to the other officers. "Good idea. Lovely drop of Rosie and all, Sergeant."

Adams blushed, causing his cheeks to clash with his orange facial hair.

"And I've taken the liberty, sir, of making appointments on your behalf with most of the doctors what work on Harley Street."

"You've – what? Appointments?"

Adams handed him a schedule. "Fastest way to get to see them, if you don't want to wait for warrants to be issued."

Kipper glanced at the list up and down. "This doesn't warrant warrants. Not at this juncture. Most of them, you say? Not all?"

Adams shifted awkwardly; he didn't like to be thought remiss. "One place was shut up, sir. Looked like nobody's been there for donkeys."

"Interesting…" said Kipper, although he was not yet sure why he might think so. "Whose is it?"

"Yes, sir."

"What?"

"You're right, sir."

"I am?"

"That's why you're the detective and I'm just a lowly sergeant."

"What are you blithering on about, man? Tell me, whose is the shut-up shop?"

"It is, sir! Got it in one, sir."

Kipper thumped the desk. The cup rattled on its saucer. "Damn it, Adams. Who is the owner?"

"I know he is."

"Who is?"

"Yes, sir!"

Kipper leapt to his feet, roaring with frustration. Adams flinched.

"Says so right here, sir," a quivering hand showed the inspector the entry in his notebook. "The shut-up shop is leased to a fellow what goes by the name of Doctor Hoo."

***

Having dismissed his cab at Baker Street, Inspector Kipper stood at the top end of Harley Street; walking the rest of the way gave him a feel for the place.

Whitechapel it ain't, he reflected as he took in the elegant terraces and gentrified townhouses. Most of the columns bore brass plaques engraved with the names of physicians, each – it seemed to Kipper – to have more letters after his name than the last. There were doctors elsewhere in London – elsewhere in the world! – but unless you'd set up shop on this particular thoroughfare, you would not be counted among the best. It was unfair and Kipper could empathise with those medics who could not find or afford space on Harley Street. It was a bit like coppers. If you said you were from Scotland Yard, people were much more impressed.

Kipper of the Yard! It had a ring to it…

But no; he was lowly John Kipper of Bow Street nick, trying his best to do his job.

He checked the list Sergeant Adams had given him. Good old Sergeant Adams. Closest I'll ever come to having a butler!

His first appointment was with a Doctor Lorrimer, F.R.C.S. Good old Sergeant Adams had taken the trouble to book appointments in order, from one end of the street to the other and then back up the other side. It was a commendable feat of organisation. Kipper resolved to buy the sergeant a pint of stout as reward for his diligence.

He climbed the five or six steps to the front door and tugged the bell-pull. A faint tinkling could be heard on the other side and before long the door was opened to reveal a pinched-faced woman in a starched grey blouse. Kipper took off his hat.

"Yes?" the woman intoned. It was like being sneered at by a cat's bum.

"I've got an appointment," Kipper, humbled by the sneer, wrung his hat in his hands.

"You must be the nine o'clock," the woman's thin lip curled. She took a step back to admit him into a hallway of chequerboard floor, dark panelled walls and a sprawling aspidistra on a stand. She pointed at a chair in an unspoken instruction for him to wait there, before gliding away. Kipper sat and reshaped his hat. Somewhere a clock ticked away the seconds, chipping away at his life, until it let out a peal of chimes, striking the hour. In an instant, the starched woman was back. She opened a door opposite Kipper's chair and ushered him through. Kipper nodded his thanks but she ignored him and withdrew.

"Do come in!" said Doctor Lorrimer, standing behind a broad desk. Kipper took in the room: more dark panelling, bookshelves crammed with important-looking volumes, potted ferns... "I won't shake your hand, if you don't mind. Not until I know what you've got, what!"

He laughed. Until he saw Kipper's warrant card.

"I'm afraid the only cure for that, Inspector, is resignation."

He offered the inspector a seat and took one himself, the leather squeaking beneath his weight.

"What's all this about, Inspector? I imagine you won't be paying for my time so I hope you will keep things brief. Time is money, you know."

"So I've heard," said Kipper. "Just a few quick questions. First off: can you tell me your whereabouts on these three nights?"

He slid a piece of paper across the blotter. Doctor Lorrimer glanced at it.

"That's easy. I keep a diary of all my engagements." He took a book from a desk drawer and leafed through it. "Ah, yes. On the first occasion, I was at the opera. Verdi. *Il Trovatore*. Do you know it?"

"Can't say I do," Kipper shook his head, wondering why anyone would want to sing about Tories.

"After which, I dined at my club. Spent the night there too. Tied it on a bit you see."

"Can't say I do," Kipper repeated. "And the other dates?"

Lorrimer turned a few pages. "Dinner with the Lord Mayor... and I was in the country. Funeral of an old friend." He paused and reflected. "I shall miss old Cacker Thomas."

Kipper decided he didn't want to know how the old friend had earned that moniker. He could eliminate Lorrimer as a suspect – dinner with the Lord Mayor would be easy enough to check. His manner toward the doctor softened; Lorrimer could assist Kipper's enquiries in another way.

"You have knives," he said. "On the premises." Seeing a frown cloud the doctor's brow, Kipper clarified, "Of a surgical nature."

"Well, yes, of course, except in the profession we tend to call them scalpels or blades."

"I should like to see them."

Doctor Lorrimer rose. "Through here."

He led the inspector through a communicating door to a room that was decked out like an operating theatre. "I only carry out simple procedures here. The lancing of boils, the stitching of minor injuries, circumcisions."

Kipper winced.

The doctor approached a lacquered cabinet and pulled out a wide, shallow drawer. The instruments within caught the light and cast gleams on the doctor's face. Kipper peered over Lorrimer's shoulder to see the tools of the doctor's trade, resting on their velvet-lined bed. The blades were of different shapes and sizes. Kipper could not imagine for what purpose many of them were fashioned. He pointed to one at the end of the row.

"What's that one there for? The one that looks like a corkscrew."

"Opening bottles of wine. It is a corkscrew. Mrs Harris…"

"Who?"

"The housekeeper. Frightful gorgon who showed you in. I'm afraid she has a fondness for the grape, if you catch my meaning, and so I keep the corkscrew in here and the key to my wine cellar close to my heart."

"Oh," said Kipper. He could not care less about the proclivities of the doctor's household staff. "Tell me, Doctor, if you were going to kill a man – or a woman, even – which one of these would you use?"

"Come, come, Inspector. Such speculation offends my belief in the Hippocratic Oath. Do no harm. Any deaths that may follow my ministrations are purely coincidental."

"Yes, of course, but say a murderer was to get his hands on these things, which one would he be better off in the using of?"

Doctor Lorrimer held his chin as he pondered. "Any of them would do the job if one put one's mind to it." He picked up an implement with a tip like an ice-cream scoop. "You could give someone a nasty gouge with this, for example."

"How about if you wanted to open somebody up, quick and easy, like, so's you can get the insides out in no time?"

The doctor looked at his visitor. "What's this about, Inspector?"

"Only asking."

A glimmer lit the doctor's eyes – from within. "This is about Foggy Jack, isn't it?"

Kipper looked put out.

"Oh, I read the papers, Inspector, like any man. I find it all rather thrilling, don't you? The police haven't a clue – the foggiest, you might say! What!"

Kipper scowled. "The murder of young women is neither thrilling nor no laughing matter neither."

Lorrimer composed himself. "No, no; I suppose not."

"So, which one?"

"What?"

"Which blade would he use?"

"Ah, I have just the thing." Lorrimer pushed the drawer shut and pulled out the one beneath. "Any basic scalpel will do the trick provided it's long enough to cut through the fat as well as the skin. Here. Oh!"

"What?"

But Kipper could see for himself. On the velvet lining of the drawer there was a gap, an indentation of where a long-bladed scalpel had been.

* * *

The rest of Kipper's interviews that morning adhered to the same pattern. All of the doctors he spoke with had attended the Lord Mayor's dinner and all had something missing from their drawers. Surgical instruments of all kinds had gone astray but only one from each practice.

The thief didn't want to be noticed, Kipper realised. Then again, there are few thieves who do. The pilfering of a scalpel here and a nasty gouging tool there would not come to light right away. Until now, Kipper thought; I've brought the thefts to light.

He scribbled a note, tore the page from his pad and sent a cabbie to deliver it to Sergeant Adams at Bow Street nick. In the meantime, he ordered all the doctors not to touch anything in their surgeries until further notice. He had a list of what had been nicked. More than enough to fill a doctor's bag.

Also, there was the matter of the shut-up surgery, the one at the end of the row, leased by – he checked his notes, a Doctor Hoo.

Well, he sounds suspicious from the start – Kipper pulled himself up sharp for such thinking. Just because the name looked foreign didn't mean the bloke was necessarily a villain. He could turn out to be another victim of the thefts and as nice as pie, could this Doctor Hoo.

Kipper was resolute; he would find a way to have a gander at Hoo's surgery by hook or by crook.

Seven

I don't know who woke up first: Doctor Hoo or the toff who'd had his leg off. All I know is it wasn't me. I'd been having a little doze myself and when I opened me minces, there they was, the doctor standing at the bench and the toff sitting up on it, dangling his legs, the old one and the new, in the air and in admiration.

"I say, old boy, you've done a marvellous job. Barely felt a thing. Can't wait to test it out, what!"

Hoo's mouth puckered ever so slightly.

"Start small," he uttered. "Toes."

"What about them?" the toff blinked. He came across as a bit thick to me, but what do I know? I haven't had the benefits of an expensive education.

Hoo's gloved fingers wiggled like he was warming up for a spot of piano practice.

"Oh, I see!" cried the toff and his face became a study in concentration with the tip of his tongue poking out. Well, the toes on his old leg – the original fixtures, you might say – they moved a treat, but the others on the new leg didn't budge at all. The toff looked at Doctor Hoo like a disappointed child on Christmas morning what's just found out his new train set is knackered. Hoo bent over the leg and with one of his spindly tools made some adjustments to the brass kneecap. Then he stood back and invited the toff to try again.

This time the new toes moved and it looked to me, even from across the laboratory, that they was better than his old ones. I don't know if you've tried wiggling your toes but they're generally not as clever as your fingers. Go on; give it a whirl. Kick your shoes off and get your Edgar Allen Poes moving.

But these new ones of the toff's they was each moving independently and it was like wave after wave, rippling across his foot. There was something, I don't know, *mechanical* about it. Well, the toff himself was fascinated but after a while he got bored and he asked the doctor to make it stop. His new toes kept moving and no matter how much he frowned at them or shook his leg or swore at them, the toff could not get them to be still. He began to panic and his hands gripped the edge of the bench and the more worked up he got, the faster his toes wiggled until they was a blur and his leg rose in the air – I don't know if it was the toff doing that or his new set of toes with a mind of their own, but I wouldn't have been surprised if he'd floated off that bench and up to the ceiling.

Doctor Hoo, by way of contrast, was calm, like a cucumber in a lab coat. He produced a hammer from somewhere about his person and approached the wayward foot with it and a stern expression (well, most of his expressions are stern ones). The look on Hoo's face must have been enough because the toff let out a squawk like a parrot sitting on an icicle and, just like that, he got his new limb under control. He sat back, panting for breath, and his boat was red and pouring with sweat.

"I suppose it will take some getting used to," the toff conceded. He gave his new toes another experimental wiggle and this time they behaved themselves as good as gold. But something was troubling Lord Twinkletoes. "I say," he said, "one does not wish to seem pernickety but could you not have found a closer match?"

Hoo frowned. I did too. The pernickety bastard.

"I mean, it's the toes. They don't quite match their counterparts on my other foot. Do you see?" He put his ankles together so that we might make better comparison. I went closer and peered from one foot to the other. Hoo remained aloof. He does that a lot.

It was true. The toes on the new foot – his left one – were longer, especially the second one, while them what he was born with was short and pink and stubby. Hoo looked as though he couldn't give a monkey's.

"Wear socks," he said and I swear I saw his shoulders twitch in a shrug.

The toff didn't like that, not one bit. He pursed his lips and pouted for a while until he could contain himself no longer and he burst out with, "Now, look here! There's something else!"

I peered closer but I was buggered if I could see it.

"The hairs!" the toff wailed. "Do you not see? The hairs on my new leg are coarse and black while those on my own leg are fine and blond. Oh, no! No, no! This will not do at all."

I don't know about Hoo but I was ready to punch this ungrateful pillock in the throat.

Hoo levelled those oblique eyes of his at the toff's and uttered a single word.

"Shave."

Well, that did it. The toff sprang from the bench in a bid to launch himself at the doctor but he still wasn't sure of his new leg and it buckled underneath him and he went down on one knee – but not for the purposes of popping the question – he went down on the brass one and his new leg bent forward at an unnatural angle and started to kick him again and again. The toff tried to scuttle away from it but everywhere Lord Beighton went, that leg was sure to go. He was like a dog being chased by its own tail. And the toff was howling and yelping like a dog and all. It was a comical sight and no mistake and it was a good job I was still wearing that little cotton mask to hide my amusement.

He pleaded – within kicks – to the doctor for help but Hoo just stood there, looking at him, like a monument to Patience or something like that, until something clicked in Lord Beighton's mind and then something clicked in his kneecap as well and he regained control of the disobedient limb. Lord Beighton lay on the floor, panting and gasping for breath. Doctor Hoo stood over him, obscuring his view of the rafters.

"Practise," he said.

"Yes, yes, I shall have to," agreed Lord Beighton.

"Pay him," said Doctor Hoo with the slightest flicker of his eyes in my direction. He stalked from the laboratory and I helped Lord Beighton to his feet. He stamped on the spot for a bit until he felt confident enough to let go of my arm.

I didn't know if I was still barred from speaking to him so I just held out my hand in the time-honoured 'pay up' gesture.

"Yes, yes, of course," Lord Beighton reached inside his coat and pulled out a chequebook. He must have been having a giraffe. I shook my head and beckoned impatiently, opening and closing my palm. This time he pulled out a purse, bulging with bees and honey. I snatched it from him and bowed low as if to say I was his humble servant, which, of course, I wasn't; only Doctor Hoo can boss me about.

I pocketed the purse and showed him to the exit, having to wait while he put his stockings, trousers and shoes back on. Which took him bleedin' ages. Not used to dressing himself, I suppose, and I wasn't going to help him on account of why should I?

At long bleedin' last I was showing him the way out to the street and slamming the door behind him before he could turn around and say something else that might get on my wick.

I strolled over to the little kitchen bit, tossing the purse and catching it, and it weren't half heavy. And, I thought for a second, this is what it feels like to be rich and to have more money than sense, like a bloke I knew called Brutus used to say.

Hoo was standing by the safe, which also doubled as the kitchen table, and he held out his hand. With reluctance, I handed over the purse and he tipped it out onto the tablecloth.

Out spilled a load of washers and nuts and bolts and stuff. There was not a single bleedin' farthing among the lot. Well, I gasped like you could have knocked me down with a feather.

"We've been diddled!" I cried, tearing off my mask. "That posh git has swindled us! Stitched us right up, good and proper, like a couple of prize kippers."

Hoo's eyes bore into mine and I couldn't read what they was saying, but it chilled me to the marrow. His lips barely parted and his moustaches barely moved but his eyes fixed me to the spot like I was a butterfly pinned in a glass box.

"Right," he said.

Eight

By hook or by crook...

The former method proved unsuccessful. Kipper had tried to pick the lock at the last house on the left but he lacked both tools and skills to do so. You have to admire your common or garden housebreaker, he reflected, to whom no lock is a barrier.

He glanced up and down the street in case such a useful character might appear out of the murk. The weather wasn't as bad as it had been; the mist was like the steam coming off of a cup of Sergeant Adams's Rosie Lee. Not thick enough, Kipper mused, to give me cover for my not-strictly-legal plan.

He looked at the brass plaque once more. It was the right place all right. The metal was tarnished and neglected, and it must be quite old, thought Kipper, because some of the lettering is worn off. But you could still make out the name, just about.

DR M. HOO

And beneath, in smaller characters: F. F. S.

"Fellow of the... um... Fellowship of Surgeons," Kipper surmised, jotting it in his notebook.

"Here, Mister," said a gruff yet high-pitched voice at his elbow. "You giving the place the onceover or what? Planning to break in? Only you must be, on account of how it's shut for business and all."

Kipper turned to find a small child of indeterminate age in clothes too large for it, covered in a liberal coating of filth and giving off a stench of ordure and cabbages.

"Get out of it," Kipper snarled, raising his hand as though to strike the child with the back of it. The child, sizing up exactly what kind of man this was, did not flinch.

"Give's a bob or I'll have the Law on you," the child held out a hand that looked like it had recently been put to use digging coal.

Kipper was aghast at the temerity of the filthy youngster. He reached into his jacket. The child's eyes widened in anticipation of easy money, only to be crestfallen when the man produced a warrant card.

"Can't read," the dirty face pouted proudly.

"It says I'm a police inspector. I am the Law."

Only then did the child cringe and begin to edge away. An idea occurred to Kipper.

"Hoi!" he called out, increasing the child's haste to be off. "Come back here."

"I ain't not done nothing!" the child protested.

"I ain't saying you have or you haven't."

"A minute ago you was telling me to get out of it."

"And now I'm telling you to come back into it. There's a tanner in it for you."

The child's face became a mask of disdain but the child's feet stopped moving.

"Make it a bob and we'll talk. But no funny business, mind."

Kipper puzzled over what the child might consider to be funny business and quickly decided he'd rather not pursue that line of enquiry.

"All right then, a bob and no funny business. Two bob if I'm satisfied."

"Hoi!" said the child.

"I mean, if you perform a certain service—"

"Hoi!"

"No! Gawd, no! I mean, can you break into this place or not?"

The child glared with suspicion. "What is this? You trying to trap me, Inspector? I breaks in and you feels my collar and crash, bang, wallop, I wakes up in Australia."

"No, no! Nothing like that. I have no intention of feeling your collar or anything else of yours, you filthy ragamuffin."

The child inhaled, indignant. "I am an urchin," the child sniffed, cut to the quick.

"I don't doubt it for a second," Kipper produced a shilling. "This is yours and another one like it when you get me into this building."

The child looked the copper up and down and then at the frontage of the property. The lure of the coin proved irresistible.

"Piece of cake."

"You can spend it on whatever you like."

The child clicked its tongue and plucked the shiny shilling from the copper's mitt. In its filthy hand the coin shone like the moon on a starless night. With the legerdemain of a conjuror, the child made the bob disappear. Reflexively, Kipper patted his pockets to check his wallet and watch were still at home.

The urchin stole up to the front door and looked back over its shoulder. "Here, there won't be no whatsits, will there? Reaper cushions?"

Kipper laughed. The child made the word sound like an undertaker's upholstery. "No, no, there won't be no repercussions. This is police business."

"But not exactly kosher."

"Just get on with it before I nick you for vagrancy."

The child harrumphed and vaulted nimbly over a railing to the basement below street level. Kipper couldn't see what was going on in the shadows but a moment later, the front door opened and the urchin bowed low.

"Do come in," the child adopted the snooty tones of a butler.

Kipper glanced around and checked no one was watching him before scurrying over the threshold. The urchin closed the door and stood with its hand out.

"You still here?" said Kipper.

"No wonder you're a bleedin' detective. Cough up and I'll be orf."

With a great show of reluctance, Kipper dropped a second shilling into the urchin's open hand. "Now piss off out of it," he snapped.

"Charming," opined the child, before tipping its filthy, shapeless hat. "Me name's Sprite, in case you ever needs me services again. Arsk anybody. Arsk for Sprite and I'll come to you."

"I don't really think that will be necess—"

But Sprite was gone.

Oh, well, Kipper shrugged. I may be down two bob but at least I'm in...

He turned around on the spot in a vestibule strewn with dust and cobwebs, wondering where to begin.

It did not occur to him until much later that he did not know whether the urchin Sprite was a boy or a girl.

***

Just as in most of the establishments he had visited, the front room was given over to a waiting area. Waiting for a duster, Kipper thought, given the state of neglect the place was in. Cobwebs were laced around the gas lamps and spanned the high ceiling like a tightrope-walkers' convention. In front of a row of severe-looking chairs, a low table was stacked with yellowing, dog-eared publications – in this respect Hoo's waiting room was exactly like all the others.

The back then...

The doctor's office too had an air of forgotten museum to it. All it needs is Miss Havisham's wedding cake, thought Kipper. No one's been here for donkeys' ears, he reckoned. He wondered if anything was missing, like all the others...

The door that communicated the office to the surgery creaked like a pig with a grievance when Kipper pushed it open. Here were all the things Kipper expected to find: the examining table, posable lamps for directed lighting and—

Hold on a minute.

It wasn't just a question of a blade missing from Doctor Hoo's operating room. The whole bleedin' cabinet was gone!

There were indentations in the rug showing where such an item of furniture had once stood. Kipper cast around for other clues but the only disturbances in the dust were those of his making.

Now, you'd think the theft of a cabinet would not go unnoticed. You'd think it would be reported... Kipper would have Sergeant Adams check with all the local nicks.

He went back to the hall. Something about the place gave him a chill down his backbone. Something hanging in the air, like fog but invisible. A bad feeling.

Kipper shivered.

There was a flight of stairs leading to the upper storeys but Kipper found the door at the top locked and unyielding to his shoulder. *Perhaps I should call that nipper back...*

That nipper what had let me in by getting into the basement...

Basement...

Kipper bounded down the stairs and looked for the door that would lead him underground. The nipper had left it ajar. Kipper wished he had given the boy or girl a third shilling for his or her trouble.

He pushed the door open and cautiously stepped down and down into the darkness. *Should have brought a lamp,* he scolded himself. *Although you hear of all sorts of explosions, what with naked flames and cellars – or am I thinking of coal mines? Something about canaries and all. If your canary stops whistling, get out of there sharpish.*

Kipper had no canary so he set to whistling for himself.

The cellar, as far as he could tell after his eyes had grown accustomed to the gloom, was empty. There was a musty smell and a chill in the air. Kipper hoped it was too cold for spiders. And rats.

He padded around, groping like a game of Blind Man's Bluff, trying to figure out the dimensions of the space. Perhaps there was a secret room or something... If this was one of them adventure serials like you'd find upstairs in them faded copies of *The Strand*, there would be.

There wasn't.

Kipper's hands found the opposite wall with its slimy coating of mould. Grimacing, he began to move sideways, like a crab moonlighting as a mime artist. A few sidesteps later, his hands found something else, something that made a hollow sound. A door.

Knock, knock, thought Kipper. Who's bleedin' there?

He patted the wooden panel until he found the doorknob, which he twisted this way and that, jiggling and pulling until the door opened.

Kipper let out a cry. A bushy, ginger beard, illuminated from beneath by a lantern, was there to greet him.

"Wotcher, Inspector," grinned Sergeant Adams. "I was just coming to find you."

Kipper swore and blasphemed. "Sergeant Adams! You tryin' to give me apoplexy or something? What the bleedin' hell are you doing here? And – how?"

"Cellars is all linked," shrugged Sergeant Adams. "A not-uncommon feature. You see, when these houses was all built—"

"Yes, yes," Kipper waved impatiently. "Spare me the bleedin' architectural history."

Adams looked a little peeved. "It's how the thief got in and out, sir."

"Thief! What do you know about the thief?"

"Got your message, sir. About fetching the fingerprint fellows from the Yard. Thought I'd come along with them. Nice bunch of lads, they is. Amazing to think how we're all different. Like snowflakes, sir, is your human fingerprint. Except they lasts a lot longer."

"Hmm," said Kipper. He snatched the lantern and made his way back to the stairs. "And have they found anything useful, this nice bunch of lads?"

It grieved Kipper to have to bring in support from Scotland Yard. He didn't want them taking over his case. And furthermore, he didn't want it to look like he couldn't cope on his Jack.

But fingerprinting was different. Fingerprinting was the latest tool in the fight against crime. And to do it you needed equipment Bow Street nick hadn't got. And specialist coppers who knew how to do it. Kipper reassured himself it was no sign of weakness to call in the fingerprinting boys.

"The place could do with a bit of a spruce-up," Adams observed when they reached the hall.

"You didn't answer my question. Have they found anything?"

"Oh, yes, sir! Not half! Of course, they has to sample the prints of all the doctors and their households and all, but when they've eliminated them, it looks like there's another set of prints that crops up at every scene. That'll be our thief, I reckon. And maybe even Foggy Jack himself, sir!"

Kipper flinched to hear the killer's nickname but it was rather exciting to think he might have a genuine lead at last. Could it be that the identity of the scourge of Whitechapel was about to be revealed?

There was a definite spring in Kipper's gait as he strode to the neighbouring building to rendezvous with his colleagues from Scotland Yard.

Nine

Well, if I've learned anything in all my dealings with Doctor Hoo it's never to pull the wool over his eyes, because he sees right through it. He sees through me like I was made of glass. And now I'm in shtuck with him and he's not happy with me.

You see, it wasn't the toff what tried to swindle him. It was me. I couldn't help myself – apart from trying to help myself to the bag of money, I mean. I've always been light-fingered and it's got me into no end of trouble, I can tell you, so you'd think I'd've learned my lesson donkeys' ago but no. The lure of the lucre proved too strong and old habits die hard and all that malarkey. Course, Hoo spotted it right away. You might think he's slower than a sloth in treacle but he clocked the second I made the switch sure enough – and I didn't even think he'd been looking in my direction. When I shut the door on the toff with his new peg and I was chucking the purse up and catching it, like I was a juggler with one ball, I pulled out a second purse from my lab coat, one with all the washers and nuts and buttons in it, and swapped them, pocketing the cash for myself. Well, I ain't got no job security in this game so I thought I'd feather me nest on the sly, like. But I reckoned without Hoo and his eagle-eyes, didn't I?

And even though that face of his didn't change, I could see the anger and betrayal in his eyes. I can read him, you see, almost as good as he can read me. His hand shot out, like a cobra's head, and grabbed me by the wrist. I cried out in surprise and then pain because he's got quite a grip on him, when he wants. He dragged me out of that little kitchen bit and up the stairs to the laboratory and I tried to get away and wriggle out of his clutches but he was liable to twist my arm off. Then his other hand brought out a cloth and before I could turn my head away, Hoo pressed the cloth to my north and south and everything faded away.

And the next thing I knew was everything was fading back and all I could see was the ceiling. I was on my back, I realised, because I'm quick like that. The ceiling of the laboratory. And I'm strapped onto the bench – it don't take me long to work that out and all.

"Hoo!" I called out. "Doctor! You there?"

He didn't answer if he was there. So I guessed he wasn't. Not that he's a chatterbox at the best of times. Which this wasn't. The best of times. Oh, I shouldn't have done it. I mean, everybody diddles their employer in some small way. A paperclip here, an extra couple of minutes on their dinner break there. But that ain't the point. You don't get one over on Doctor Hoo. You just don't.

I tried to get free of the rubber tubing that was holding me down but I knew before I started there was fat chance of that. Hoo had tied me down good and proper. I didn't know why. Why didn't he just give me the elbow on the spot? Or, if he wanted to punish me, why hadn't he – I don't know – cut me up a bit or done away with me altogether? He's a funny old bird is Doctor Hoo. Full of surprises.

I lay back and cursed myself. What a prize pilchard I am! I have been and gone and ruined everything. What am I going to do now? Go back to the streets? If Hoo lets me go, of course, which, given my current predicament, don't seem too likely.

My head was pounding. Whatever was on that cloth don't half leave you with a nasty hangover. My throat was parched and all. I could've murdered an acrobat.

By which I mean I could do with a drink. You know: acrobat. Tumbler. I ain't into killing circus folk. Nor nobody else, come to that.

It was the circus what brought me and Hoo together. I was in shtuck with him then. He only bleedin' caught me sneaking in, didn't he? Well, I couldn't afford to buy a ticket, could I? I was a kid on the streets and all the money I could get went to some geezer called Brutus who put me up and other kids like me (and there's plenty of them) in a tenement in the East End. If you didn't pay, well, I dread to think what Brutus would do to you, but there was some kids I never saw again and I don't reckon it was on account of being adopted by no kindly old benefactor, do you?

Well, Hoo caught me by the ankles just as I was crawling under the canvas to get into the big top. Hooked me with the handle of his brolly, he did, and yanked me right out. Well, I'd never been so scared in all me born days – and I'd seen Brutus pie-eyed and slashing about with a cutthroat razor one night – because he's tall is Doctor Hoo and with me only a kid and down at ground level, he seemed even taller. I looked up past his umbrella and up his long coat – he was like a tree trunk and his face was somebody's kite stuck in the top branches with a topper stuck on it for good measure. I tried to scurry away but he gave his brolly a yank, whisking me off the ground and into the air and his hand shot out and grabbed me by the throat and he pulled me face next to his and I thought, this is it, he's going to bite my head orf. Only he don't. He looked me in the eyes and I couldn't look away and it's like he could see right through me, right down to the holes in my sock (I only had the one at the time) and then it stopped. And I see something change on his face, although it might have been a trick of the light. He put me back on the ground but he held onto my hand and he marched me away from the tent.

No show for me that night, then.

He took me away from the tent, and the show, and the noise and the crowd, but the funny thing was I knew he wasn't going to hurt me. I don't know how I knew it; maybe I had seen something in his eyes and all. We go past a few caravans and wagons with cages on. And it flashed across my mind that he was going to feed me to the lions or something. All because I tried to get in without paying? It didn't seem reasonable. But I knew deep down he wouldn't. His grip on my hand didn't hurt. It was firm but, I don't know, it was a little bit comforting as well. I couldn't remember the last time somebody had held my hand. I don't think it had ever happened before. I was glad of it, I suppose. To have my hand held by a grown-up, to have a grown-up taking charge of me. There is a first time for everything. And it didn't even matter that he was wearing gloves. To me it felt like someone was looking after me for once in my life.

He took me to a wagon that was painted up and must have been rather pretty when it was first done, only by now it was faded and tatty and a bit sad-looking. There was a banner across the top but I couldn't read it, could I? I ain't never had no schooling. He stopped and pointed at it.

"Hoo," he said.

"What are you, a bleedin' owl?"

He placed his free hand on his chest and said it again.

"Oh, that's your name! Well, I'm Deacus. Damien Deacus. Pleased to meet you, Mister Hoo."

He shook his head. He pointed at the pictures on the side of the wagon. Pictures of him, standing over people, with flashes coming out of his eyes. I didn't get it. Well, the drawings weren't much cop.

"Doctor," he said, when he'd given up on me ever cottoning on.

"Who is?"

"Yes," he said.

He took me inside and lit a lamp. I hadn't never seen anything like it. It was like, I don't know, a museum on wheels. There was shelves everywhere and on them shelves was bottles and jars with all sorts of strange things in them: animals in coloured liquids, like they'd been pickled – animals the like of which I ain't never seen. And there was gadgets with workings like clocks and puppets, all sorts of puppets. I was quite taken with the puppets on account of I ain't never had no toys to call me own.

Doctor Hoo gestured, inviting me to touch the puppets, and I picked up a clown and waved his arm a little bit. Then a copper holding a truncheon. I picked him up and all and made him bash the clown on the head. And Doctor Hoo made a noise and I thought he was angry only when I looked at him I could tell he was laughing.

I could see too that the door to the wagon was wide open. He hadn't locked it, hadn't even shut it. It was like he knew I wouldn't run off.

It did occur to me. To have it away on me plates, taking a couple of them puppets with me. I'm fast, you see. You have to be if you want to keep out of reach of the peelers. Hoo moved further in, to show me something else, and giving me a clear shot at the door. I could go. Just go, taking the clown and the copper with me, one for me and one for Squeaker who is a little nipper I sometimes bunk with, and he didn't look like he would even try to stop me.

But, for some reason, I didn't go. I stayed where I was, and looked around at all the stuff he'd got in his wagon.

"Here," I said. "What do you do? In the circus, I mean. What's your act?"

He picked up a gadget, a circle on a stick, and the circle was painted with black and white spirals on it and he gave it a whirl and the spirals twisted before my eyes. He pointed it at his own face and pretended to go into a trance.

"Oh!" I laughed. "You're a wossname. A nipnotist."

He bowed and put the stick back where it belonged.

"And you do puppets on the side?"

He made a gesture that was neither yes nor no. He beckoned me to a table. There was a puppet of a dog, lying on its side. Doctor Hoo clicked his fingers at it – not easy to do when you're wearing gloves, I reckon – and the little dog sat up. It whirred like the insides of a clock and turned its head and I swear it looked right at me, because its tongue came out and it yipped at me. Doctor Hoo clicked his fingers again and the dog lay down again.

I dared to touch it.

"It's warm!" I said, stroking its coat with my finger. I tried clicking but the dog took no notice. Only Doctor Hoo could bring it to life. I looked at him with wonder, this peculiar man, stooping in a wagon he was too tall for, his face like a carved mask, and his work all around him, and I thought I'd never seen anybody like him, there was nobody like him in all the world, and I knew I didn't want to go nowhere else. I wanted to stay with him and find out more, and play with his marvellous toys.

"Yes," he said.

"Yes what?" I said. Because I was sure I hadn't said nothing out loud.

"Stay," he said, gesturing at the wagon.

"Well, well, well," said a voice from the doorway and I didn't need to turn around to see who it was. Brutus. "Ain't this a pretty picture!"

"How did you find me?" I said, backing away so there was a table between us. Brutus stepped in – he was never one to stand on ceremony – and he pulled something from around his back and threw it at the floor.

"I'm sorry, Deacus!" cried the thing and I saw it was Squeaker, sobbing his little heart out.

"Last time I tell you nothing," I said and it sounded harsh when I said it, and perhaps I should have been kinder because you never know what's going to be the last thing you say to somebody, do you?

Brutus lifted his leg and brought his hobnail boot down on my little matey like he was an insect in his path. And I heard a crack, a sickening crack, and Squeaker was dead, his head hanging loose and at the wrong angle. Like one of Doctor Hoo's puppets. Brutus grinned, treating us to a view of the crooked black stumps of his teeth.

"Turns out you can't trust nobody these days," he said, reaching for me. The stench of him, all piss and gin, filled the wagon. "You're coming with me or you'll get the same as that little rat."

He spat on Squeaker's body.

"I ain't!" I screamed. "I ain't going nowhere. Am I, Doctor?"

"O-ho!" And it's like Brutus saw Doctor Hoo for the first time. "Who's going to stop me? This bunch of firewood?"

Hoo didn't speak. He reached for that circle on a stick thing and held it in front of Brutus's mush.

"What's this? A lollipop?"

And then the circle began to turn. Faster and faster and Brutus couldn't take his eyes off of it. And Doctor Hoo's other hand is making signs in the air. Signs of walking, signs of claws. And Brutus, looking dazed and stunned, spins around on his heels and marches out of the wagon.

"Where's he going?" I said. But of course, Hoo didn't tell me.

I rushed to the doorway and watched Brutus stride away, like a clockwork soldier. I was glad to see the back of him – it's his best feature, apart from his absence – but what happened next I was not expecting. He went right up to the lions' cage and climbed on top. The lions was asleep. He undid the lock – there was a trapdoor on the top for when the cats needed feeding, I shouldn't wonder – and Brutus drops himself through it and into the cage. Well, the lions was wide awake by this point and growling and roaring – I can be moody too if my sleep's interrupted – and then they catch wind of him and how could they not? And that's it for him. Doctor Hoo pulled me, but gently, inside and shut the door so's I wouldn't have to witness the lions making a meal out of that brute Brutus.

"Well, that was unexpected," I said, marvelling at the spinning circle.

Hoo put it away and then he stooped and picked up poor Squeaker, who ain't never had no luck in all his short life, and he put him on the table. And I couldn't help thinking of all the other nippers back in the tenement. They was free, weren't they? But who would come next? Who would be the next Brutus taking advantage of them? And would he be worse?

Hoo picked up some tools and some little wheels and I guessed what he was going to do.

"No!" I cried and I slapped the tool from his hand. It was a bold move but I was upset, wasn't I? "You ain't going to make no puppet out of my friend."

And Hoo looked at me, reading me, and I guess he saw something that made him change his mind.

He wrapped Squeaker in a cloth and we took him outside and buried him in a corner of the field. I was sorry to say goodbye to him; he was my only friend. But on the bright side, he was away from all this worldly suffering, which is something no kid should ever have to deal with, and I wouldn't have to worry about leaving him behind.

"Secret," said Hoo when we was back in the wagon.

"Not half," I agreed. Even though he was only an urchin, was Squeaker, the coppers don't like it when they turns up dead. It's like the only time anybody cares about the likes of us.

Hoo hitched up a bottle of sauce to the wagon and it clip-clopped us away from there, away from the circus, before the show was even over.

"What's his name?" I said. "The horse."

"Never introduced," said Hoo, flicking the reins. It took me a while but it dawned on me that he had made a joke.

We spent a couple of years riding around, visiting villages and what-not in the back of beyond. I learned a few tricks of the trade and Hoo let me work some of the puppets because I was good at giving them voices and making the kids laugh. And while he was doing his bit with the grown-ups, making them fall asleep and cluck about like chickens and I don't know what, I would go into the crowd with me cap held out so they could pay for their entertainment. I might have said it before but old habits die hard and so what if I helped myself to a wallet here and a handkerchief there, I wasn't hurting nobody. Until Hoo found out about it and he pinned me with them eyes of his – he never needed to use his spinning circle on me. And I said all right, all right, I wouldn't do it no more and I even went around the crowd putting stuff back. I think I got all the stuff back in the right pockets and if I didn't I hope they just thought it was all part of the show.

After that, we stopped doing the villages and come back into London where Hoo rented himself a gaff on Weymouth Street. Proper swanky and no mistake. And I said, here, wouldn't you rather be around the corner on Harley Street and he give me one of his long, cold stares, what I guessed meant No. And he put away his puppets, locked them away on the top floor, and I was made to wear posh clobber like I was a butler or something and it was my job to welcome people at the door and show them in when the doctor was ready to see them. It was easy work but it weren't half boring, I can tell you.

He made a lot of brass on account of all his clients was posh gits and toffs. He used his spinning circle on them to convince them their aches and pains was all gone. Worked like a charm, it did.

At night, he taught me to read. Or rather he stood over me until I taught myself, sounding out the letters, putting the sounds together to make the words. It weren't easy but I picked it up, sooner rather than later on account of me not being as thick as I look. And it was all going well but of course, nothing ever goes well forever. Something always goes wrong, don't it? Something always happens to spoil things.

Remind me to tell you about the Lord Mayor's dinner.

Ten

Kipper did something he hadn't done in a long time. He went home. He rented an attic flat in Fulham, a tiny space with a bed, a washstand, and a chair on which he draped his clothes – and there were not many of them. It wasn't cheerful but it was cheap and the landlady, Mrs Plum, liked having a copper in the house because it kept her other lodgers in check, even though that copper was hardly ever there. Kipper was a spectral figure, a bogeyman whose name Mrs Plum invoked should anyone prove too rowdy, drunk, or behind with the rent.

The creak of his foot on the lowermost stair brought Mrs Plum from her ground floor apartment like a jack from its box.

"Hoo-hoo, Inspector!" she flagged him down with a handkerchief. "Have you caught the bastard?"

Kipper, frozen in the act of climbing the stairs, frowned at his landlady. "And which bastard might that be, Mrs P? City is crawling with them."

"You know…" she leant toward him and lowered her voice to a conspiratorial whisper. "*Him.* Foggy Jack!"

"No!" said Kipper sharply. "Not yet."

"Oh." Mrs Plum straightened; she didn't like his tone. She would have to tell the Inspector about him – oh, damn it, he *is* the Inspector. "Only I just thought, what with on account of your being here. Because you said you wouldn't rest until you'd catched him."

"Do I look rested?" snapped Kipper. "Mrs P, you know and I know I am not at liberty to discuss with you the progress or otherwise of my investigations. I've just come back for a bit of a kip, a wash and brush-up before I hurl myself back into the fray."

"Oh. Sorry I'm sure." Her fingers toyed with the handrail. "I've a lovely bit of stew on the go if you'd like some. Fresh bread and all."

She looked up at him with lonely widow's eyes. Kipper's stomach rumbled audibly.

"That settles it!" she laughed. "It'll be ready in an hour." She pouted coyly and twisted a lock of her silver hair. "I could bring it up…"

"No, no!" Kipper said, a little too quickly. "I'll come down. An hour, you said. That'll be lovely."

Despite his fatigue, he bounded up the stairs two or three at a time, all the way up to the top of the house. He shucked off his overcoat and threw it and himself onto the narrow bed, pulling his hat over his face. Kip would not come. He was a Kipper who could not kip. His mind raced through the facts of the case so far, over and over, until everything blurred together like a broken kaleidoscope.

One thing he was sure of: this Doctor Hoo figure had something to do with something…

"Coo-ee! Inspector!" Mrs Plum sang from the other side of the door. "Dinner's ready."

Kipper groaned. The doorknob rattled. He sprang from the bed in a panic. If that woman got in, he'd never get her out.

"I'll be right down!" he called back.

"Rightio," she replied. He listened to her padding away. When he was sure he was safe, he undressed, washed his face, hands and armpits and put on a clean shirt. One thing about Mrs P: she provided an excellent laundry service and kept his ewer filled with clean water.

With fresh face and clearer mind, he skipped down the stairs. He rapped on the door to Mrs Plum's living room with his knuckle.

"Come *in*!" she trilled from the other side. Steeling himself to repel all boarders – or rather, all landladies – Kipper went inside.

The room was in darkness, save for a single lamp at the centre of the table. There were two place settings – Kipper's heart sank to see they would be dining alone, but the delicious aroma emanating from the earthenware tureen was irresistible.

"Do have a seat," said Mrs Plum, gesturing at the only other visible chair. Kipper pulled it out and sat.

"What's this then, Mrs P? A séance?"

"Hardly. Just a humble meal between friends." She ladled a steaming, lumpy helping into a bowl and held it out. "Wait until you get your gnashers into my dumplings."

Kipper cleared his throat. "Look, Mrs P—"

"Call me Ophelia."

"Listen, Mrs O. This is all jolly decent of you and all but…"

The dish was withdrawn. "Don't flatter yourself, Johnny." She slammed the bowl on the table causing a tide of stew to surge over the rim and onto the cloth. "I don't know; you treats a man nice, with kindness and respect on account of him being a copper and bringing a bit of prestige into the house, and he ain't got no wife to look after him, and he thinks you wants to get your claws into him and all manner of indecency, what I ain't never even dreamt of."

She blew her nose into her handkerchief. Kipper was guilt-stricken. He rose from his chair.

"I'm sorry, me old duck," he said. "Look: I'll take charge, shall I?" He took up the ladle. "You let me do the work for a change." He whisked a tea towel off a small basket. "Bread roll, modom?"

Mrs Plum giggled like a girl forty years her junior. "Don't mind if I do," she simpered.

Gawd help me, thought Kipper.

They were interrupted by thunderous knocking at the front door. Mrs Plum muttered something colourful and stood, dropping her napkin onto her place mat. She left the room and presently Kipper heard a voice he recognised. He joined Mrs P and the visitor in the hall.

"Adams! What is it, man?"

The sergeant nodded a salute that was also an apology. "Ever so sorry, sir, to intrude on your little soiree." He looked askance at the landlady and lowered his voice. "Only there's been developments."

The inspector's eyes slid sideways to Mrs Plum, who was doing her best to appear aloof, patting hairpins back into place. Clearly, she was hanging on their every word.

"I'll get my coat," Kipper announced and bounded up the stairs.

***

Adams brought Kipper up to speed with the latest developments during the cab ride back to Bow Street. The fingerprint boys had isolated a set of prints common to every crime scene, belonging to none of the doctors nor any of their staff. The team was checking through the records to see if the prints matched those of any known villain.

"Then we'll know who we're looking for," Adams concluded, adding quite unnecessarily in Kipper's opinion, "Great bunch of lads, them Scotland Yard boys."

"Ah," said Kipper. "But what if they don't find a match? What then, eh?"

"Ah, well," Adams combed his beard with his fingers. "That's just it, sir. Any suspects we bring in, we takes prints off of them and then see if they matches."

"I see."

"They'll show you how to do it."

"Who will?"

"The Scotland Yard boys."

"Show me what?"

"How to take somebody's prints."

"I'm not a complete idiot."

"Yes, sir – I mean, No, sir."

They arrived at the nick. Kipper was dismayed to find it had been annexed by that great bunch of lads from good old Scotland

Yard. The air in his office was thick with smoke from their pipes. Might as well stay outside in the peasouper, he coughed.

"Hail, Johnny! Well met!" A grinning face emerged from the murk along with a hand for Kipper to shake – which Kipper studiously ignored. "Bigby of the Yard," said the face, teeth clenched around the stem of his malodorous pipe. Bigby's hair reeked of Macassar oil. Revolting, Kipper shuddered.

The unshaken hand clapped Kipper on the shoulder. "You've arrived in the nick, what! I say! That's rather good, isn't it? Arrived in the nick – as in the nick of time, and nick as in police station, as I believe the vulgarians call it." He addressed the room. "I say, lads! Did you hear that? The inspector here has arrived IN THE NICK!"

Three heads bobbed up from desks. "Haw! Haw!" they chorused.

"Ha! Ha!" laughed Sergeant Adams. Kipper shot him a murderous look.

"I do believe," Bigby's eye crinkled in a wink and his finger tapped the side of his nose, "we may have identified your man." He smirked and awaited a reaction from Kipper. The one he got was not the amazement and/or gratitude he had perhaps expected. Instead, the inspector appeared to be doing a rather good impression of a kettle trying not to boil.

"Oh, really?" Kipper managed to keep his voice relatively even. "Then who the bloody hell is it?"

Bigby beamed. He held out a hand. A sheet of paper arrived in it having been passed from great lad to great lad around the room. Kipper reached for it but Bigby snatched it back again. Childishly, in Kipper's view. Bigby held the paper top and bottom like a town crier's scroll. He cleared his throat and made an announcement.

"Hear ye, hear ye, hear ye!"

The great bunch of lads chortled.

"Let it be known that the set of prints discovered in every property on Harley Street belongs to petty thief and known ne-er-do-well, one Damien Deacus."

Kipper looked stunned; Bigby was gratified by the effect of his revelation. He rolled up the paper and tapped the inspector's shoulder with it.

"There you go, Johnny. As easy as that. Amazing what the application of modern science can do, what!"

"Give me that!" Kipper snatched the paper and unfurled it. "And there's no mistake?"

"None whatsoever," Bigby grinned. "He's our man. He stole the surgical instruments, no doubt about it. And he's very probably using them to murder dollymops. He's very possibly Foggy Jack."

The great bunch of lads cheered.

"No, mate," said Kipper. He tore the paper in half and the halves in half again before letting the pieces fall to Bigby's feet. "It ain't Deacus. I'm telling you. I mean, he might have nicked the blades all right—"

"He did!"

"But he ain't the killer. It ain't possible."

"Oh?" Bigby chewed on his pipe. "And you know this for a fact, do you?"

"Oh, yeah." It was Kipper's turn to smirk in triumph. "On account of that tea leaf and toe rag Damien Deacus being brown bread and buried. So there."

Eleven

It can be a disconcerting turn of events to wake up with another man's hand on your winkle. I tried to brush it away, only the hand I used wasn't mine either. Startled, ain't the word. I stared at the hands, holding them above my head. They were attached to arms, but they weren't my arms. And those arms was – I threw back the sheet – attached to my shoulders! Brass fittings a bit like that toff's nifty new kneecap joined the arms to my body.

I checked. I counted. My old arms was gone! Replaced by this new pair. I tried to pinch myself to make sure it wasn't a dream but I couldn't get the fingers to work properly. What the hell?

Doctor Hoo had knocked me out with his handkerchief and then swapped my arms! Why would he do such a thing? And without a 'by your leave'? I wasn't in the market for new arms and as soon as I set eyes on him, I'd tell him I wanted the old ones back, thank you very much.

I got off the operating table, which was no easy feat considering my new Chalk Farms was just hanging there, like meat in a butcher's storeroom. I gave myself the onceover to see if anything else had been exchanged without my consent. It all seemed present and correct and how I remembered it. Oh, why would Hoo do this to me?

The new arms was thicker than mine, more muscular, so they had that in their favour. Made my chest look all the punier though. And my hands. Bigger, broader, stronger. I tried to pick up something and had to concentrate to get the unfamiliar fingers to budge. Now I knew how that toff had felt with his new peg. The effort was making me sweat but I was determined to master them so that, when I saw Hoo, I could demand me old ones back or bleedin' strangle him with these.

As far as skin tone went, he'd picked a good match, I have to give him that. And the craftsmanship of them little brass gizmos was exquisite as the fanciest fob watch. I could just about hear the little gears at work as I experimented moving me new chalks this way and that. With a shirt and jacket on, you wouldn't know they was there.

Hold on a minute. I wasn't getting used to the idea already, was I? Sod that for a game of soldiers.

Perhaps my old head was still woozy from whatever Hoo drugged me with on his handkerchief.

I sat down and held my head in my hands – and that felt strange and all, and I ended up staring at my new brass bands all over again. They're supposed to be the most familiar things in the world, ain't they? The backs of your hands. But these was foreign objects. Every hair, every mole, line and wrinkle. It was like poring over a map of a city you've never heard of, let alone been to.

Mind reeling, I went back to the operating table. I climbed on it and lay back, curling up into a little ball with my new arms hugging me like a stranger's embrace. I needed to give the drugs time to wear off. That's all this was. I'd be able to think more clearly then.

While my new arms was clinging to me, in my head I was clinging to the hope that all this was some weird hallucination brought about by Hoo and his bleedin' hanky.

***

Oh, yeah, I was going to tell you about the night of the Lord Mayor's dinner. He holds it every year apparently, for the luminaries of the medical profession. Doctors to you and me. Turns out he's throwing dinners all year round for somebody or other. Doctors one week, the Admiralty the next. The Royal Society of Chimney

Bleedin' Sweeps. Perhaps His Worship has an aversion to home cooking, I don't know.

Anyway, one year on the night of the party, I was under special instruction from Doctor Hoo and, well, when he says jump, you don't ask how high is a Chinaman? He gave me a list, sort of like a shopping list, except I weren't going to pay for nothing off it. And as well as words there was pictures of the items I was sent to find – which proved very handy, I must say. I mean, could you have recognised a left-handed *trephine* or a spring-loaded *ecraseur* or even a crank-handled *scarificator* if you only read the name? No. I didn't think so. Doctor Hoo was replenishing his cabinet of medical instruments – the cabinet he'd had me hump across town like it weren't nothing.

And so, armed with this list and a bunch of homemade-looking keys, I was despatched to his old Harley Street office, where nobody hadn't been for ages. I felt highly honoured – I didn't even know he had one. But the shine wore off when I saw the state of the place! I hope he weren't expecting me to run round with a feather duster.

The keys was all for the cellars – apart from a couple that I'll come to in a bit – on account of the cellars all being interconnected for some reason. Something to do with servants, I reckon, or tradesmen's deliveries; I don't know. Doctor Hoo had made them keys himself and it was my job to go from building to building and get my mitts on everything what was on the list. Only I wasn't to take no more than one thing from each place, so that their absence wouldn't be noticed right away, or something; I don't know. I don't understand what goes on in Hoo's mind no more than a goat understands the workings of Big Bleedin' Ben. But I did what I was told. I enjoyed it. It was quite exciting, sneaking into them offices after dark. They was all out, you see, the doctors, at the dinner. All I had to watch out for was the servants, only most of them had taken the night orf. There was one place though, the last one in the row, where something happened that made me nearly fill my round the houses. I got into the place all right, with me bag of swag clinking over my shoulder, and I found the cabinet all right – them doctors displayed a great lack of imagination when it came to interior design – only I couldn't get the bleedin' thing open. The key didn't fit. I tried the lot and then, sweating, I dropped the keyring and it lands on the carpet so there's no sound. Phew, I thinks, and I bends down to pick it up, only to bump my head on the cabinet when I straightens up again. I just about managed to stifle the swear what was trying to burst forth by clamping my hand over my north and south. I froze. I didn't even dare rub my head. I listened. If there was anybody in the house, they could have heard the bump if not the swear.

Nothing.

But I gave it a few more minutes just in case, holding my breath. And I thought I'd better get a wiggle on in case the doctor come home from the party.

Still nothing.

And I was about to give the cabinet another go and I'm sorting through the keys and I'm aware of time running out, when I hears a thud coming from the corridor. Seconds later, the door is opening and somebody's coming in. But they ain't got no lamp, no candle, nothing. My first thought – well, my second after I'd done a little mental swear – was that it was another burglar. I nips across the room, sharpish, and hid myself behind a gigantic potted plant. I watched as the somebody came in and it's a woman and she's stumbling and bumbling around, muttering to herself. She's holding a bottle by the neck and she takes a swig of it every other step.

She's Jumbo's trunk! Well, you don't have to be no doctor to diagnose that. She heads straight – straight as she can manage – for the cabinet and while I'm thinking 'Hoi! I was here first!' she gives it a bash on the side. Blow me if a drawer don't slide out of its own accord! She pulls something from her apron pocket and it's a bit of a struggle because it gets caught but she pulls it out and holds it up and sneers at it. It's one of the doctor's tools, it looks like, I can see the shape of it – it's like a bleedin' corkscrew! And I don't want to imagine what a doctor might do to you with such a thing!

She lies it in the drawer like she's putting a tiny child to bed and turns around, muttering to herself. I catch a few words. "I'll show him" and "wine cellar" … and she totters out on her way. I ain't never been so pleased to see the back of somebody.

And the thing is, she's left the drawer open! Good girl!

When all was quiet, I nipped over to the cabinet and I see that the thing she put in is a corkscrew all right. Well, it's none of my business if she's sneaking around helping herself to bottles of the doctor's plonk while he's out the house. But she's done me a favour so I'm of a mind to do the same for her. I found the thing I wanted – a nickel-plated dilator thing what was only a little less twisty than the corkscrew – and then I pushed the drawer shut, to save the housekeeper or whoever it was from an embarrassing interview with her employer.

I was just closing the cellar door behind me when I heard a carriage pulling up outside.

Phew ain't the half of it!

***

I got back to Hoo's place and laughed like a drain. I had only bleedin' gone and done it. I was worried I might have lost the knack on account of not being out house-breakin' since my days in the tender care of Brutus, when Squeaker would stay outside the gaff I was robbin' and give out a squeak if somebody was coming. I learned to creep around without making a sound, keeping my ears attuned for Squeaker's squeak.

Poor Squeaker.

But this was a time for celebrating. Hoo was going to be tickled pink with me, he was. Like I say, I don't know what his game was when he could have just bought the bleedin' things in one fell swoop but another thing I've learned is that Hoo don't like it if I asks too many questions. He's not one for explaining himself.

I tried to keep my spirits up and hang on to the feeling of elation and relief but it's like trying to keep a cup of tea warm. Eventually it goes cold. Where the bleedin' hell was Hoo? Why wasn't he there to congratulate me – and perhaps tip me a bit of a bonus? I got bored with waiting. And there was nothing to do in that empty place, apart from the faded magazines and it was too dark to have a squint at them; I was under strict instruction not to light a candle in case it was seen from the street.

And then I remembered them keys. Do you remember them keys? I said there was a couple of keys that I hadn't used in my burglaries. Well, I thought, I could do with another challenge. Time to find out where these keys fit and what secrets they was guarding.

It didn't take long to search the ground floor. There weren't nothing there with a keyhole only the doors I had already used, so a few minutes later I was up the stairs and in front of the door, the locked door, that separated Hoo's public practice rooms from the rest of the house.

Two keys, one lock. Got it first guess. I was on fire that night! Everything was going my way.

I pushed the door open. It didn't even creak but I held me breath all the same. I prepared myself for my shins to locate any and all furniture in my path as I groped around in the dark. There was a squeak! And my heart flipped on account of me thinking it was Squeaker, sounding the alarm, but me head knew it wasn't on account of people not coming back from the grave (well, apart from me, of course) and I thought it was a mouse. Good luck, mouse, finding something to nibble on in this empty house. But it weren't no mouse; it was the floorboards beneath my boots. I felt a right silly sausage.

By this time, my minces was a bit used to the dark and I could see deeper shadows in the corners, with straight edges indicating they was cupboards or cabinets or what-have-you. And cupboards or cabinets or what-have-you might have locks and one of them locks might fit the last remaining key in my sweaty brass band.

So, I groped about like a blind man in a foreign country until I came to the first square shadow and I patted it all over like it was the family dog, and I quickly worked out it was a bookcase with books on it. What them books was, I couldn't tell you. Perhaps if I'd been fed more carrots back in me misspent childhood, I might have been able to pick out a few titles but old Brutus didn't go in for providing a balanced diet. There was the smell of old books about them, which is oddly comforting, although I could guess that what they contained would be the opposite of comforting, knowing the kind of thing Doctor Hoo went in for.

I moved onto the next piece and it was flat at the sides and across the top but smooth and curved at the front. It was a whatsit, weren't it, a bureau? A writing-desk to you and me. And writing-desks have locks, don't they? My fingers felt around for the little plaque with the keyhole in it. The excitement was building up inside me again, because this was just another burglary, wasn't it? Burgling my boss! Oh, he'd murder me if he found out. Only it weren't exactly burgling, was it? On account of I was only having a peep, just to satisfy my curiosity and give me something to do on account of him keeping me waiting around. So in a way it was his fault.

I could barely get the key in the hole on account of my fingers fumbling with excitement and I thought it weren't going to fit but then I took a breath and calmed down a bit. In it went, like a pizzle up a dollymop. There was a faint little click and I knew I was in. I rolled up the curved front and my hands explored the little cave inside. Papers and shelves, pencils and inkwells. All this I found by touch alone. And there was a book, quite a hefty one and all, bulging with papers and bookmarks. I pulled it out and gave it a good feel. I moved to the window in the hope of some moonlight but all I could see was that there was writing on the pages – handwriting, I mean – but I couldn't make head nor tail of it. It would have to wait until morning. Perhaps at dawn's crack, I might have a better chance.

Speaking of dawn, it couldn't be far off and still no sign of Doctor Hoo. A cold thought popped into my head and trickled down my spine. What if I'd got it wrong? What if he'd told me to meet him somewhere else and in my excitement I'd forgotten all about it? He wouldn't be too happy with me, would he?

I wracked my brain trying to recall his words – and there weren't many of them to recall: Here are keys, here is list, get things on list, wait…

I couldn't recall anything after that. Perhaps he didn't say no more.

Wait…

So, I waited. I curled up in a corner with my coat wrapped around me and that book clutched to my chest like a shield. And I nodded off, all my energy drained away. I was tired to the bone, I was. Dead to the world.

But not so out of it I couldn't wake up when them floorboards gave out the tiniest squeak.

And there he was, towering over me, like a yellow tree with a face like a pissed-off jack-o'-lantern, was dear old Doctor Hoo. He held out a gloved hand but not to help me up. He wanted the book.

"Morning!" I said trying to be cheerful and breezy like I ain't done nothing wrong but the word caught in my throat. I coughed to clear it away.

The hand was still there, insistent. I got to my feet, my knees and back aching like I was a little old man. I got my first look at the book proper and I wanted to hang on to it and have a proper butcher's inside but Hoo's fingers closed around it and we had a bit of a tug-o'-war over it, until I let it go.

His eyes stared into me but I stared back for as long as I could stand it.

And then to my surprise – he is full of surprises is Doctor Hoo – he opens the book and shows it to me, turning the pages slowly. I peered at it but I couldn't make no sense of it. It was handwriting but I couldn't make out a word. Now, I'm not one to judge on account of my own handwriting being, well, nothing to write home about, but this lot was unreadable because it weren't English. This was all dots and squiggles of a different kind. Like it was all foreign. Chinese, I shouldn't wonder.

"Shorthand," said Doctor Hoo and I thought he was being fresh so I thought about calling him big nose or something like that but I could tell he wasn't in the mood.

He turned another page and there was clippings from newspapers stuck to it, and these I could read because they was in The Queen's English. I peered closer. They was all about the Lord Mayor's Dinner from years ago, judging by the date. UPROAR, said one! SCANDAL, said another!

I leant in to have a squint at the small print and slam! Hoo snapped the book shut, trapping my hooter like a mouse in a trap.

I swore and I squirmed; he let me go. There was a glimmer in his eye; he was enjoying himself. He strode over to the bureau and put the book back inside. Then he rolled it shut and twisted the key – I'd left it in the bleedin' lock, hadn't I? And he took the key out and slipped it into his pocket.

"Why?" I protested. "Why let me have a sniff at the rabbit and then lock the hutch?"

Of course, he didn't answer on account of him never explaining nothing.

"List," he said, holding out his hand again. I fished out the piece of paper and handed it over. "Things?"

"In a bag. Downstairs. I did it. I got the lot."

He nodded and that's how I could tell he was pleased with me, and why he was being so lenient with me about poking around in his drawers.

He stalked out of that room and I knew I had to follow or else he would lock me in. He don't say much, don't Doctor Hoo, but somehow I can read him like a book what ain't shut away in no writing-desk.

***

Well, that was then. Here I am now, recovering from arm-replacement surgery what I didn't even want, and waiting to see what the bleedin' hell Hoo had got in store for me next. Perhaps he took my arms off as punishment because he caught me trying to pull a fast one with the toff's money? They do that in some countries, you know. But then, why did he give me new ones?

Because my nicking stuff suits him sometimes. Like that cabinet's worth of instruments I was telling you about.

I just don't get it.

Twelve

Kipper was both amazed at and impressed by the speed at which the lads from Scotland Yard got things done. But he was buggered if he was going to let them know that. If it was me, he reflected, it would take weeks of begging and cajoling my superiors but no, here we are, just a few hours later, standing in the cemetery, watching two men with shovels dig up the final resting place of that toe rag, Damien Deacus.

Kipper felt like a bit of a spare part. They wouldn't even let him hold a lantern. He stamped his feet on the cold, damp earth and rubbed his hands together. The Scotland Yard lads were more suitably attired. They must exhume bodies all the time.

Honour was at stake. What was warming Kipper's cockles was the anticipation of seeing the smiles drop from their smug faces when the corpse was revealed to be where he'd said it was. Then they'd see. Then they'd see he was as good as they were.

The edge of a shovel struck something – but it didn't sound like the wood of a coffin lid.

"O-ho!" said Bigby. "What have we here?"

"Dead body," said one of the diggers; it came as no surprise to him.

"Hold up," said the other. "Make that two. There's another one in here and all."

Bigby sent Kipper a quizzical look. "Did your friend Deacus have a Siamese twin?" He puffed on his pipe.

"Not my friend!" Kipper muttered. He peered over the edge of the excavation. Two faces peered up out of the dirt, contorted with pain and blackened from fire. Kipper backed away – but not too quickly in case it was interpreted as weakness.

Bigby directed the removal of the bodies. Moments later, they were laid out on the ground on tarpaulin sheets.

"Which one?" Bigby chewed his pipe.

"Which one what?" blinked Kipper.

"Which one is Deacus?"

"Um…" Kipper forced himself to look closely. Damien Deacus had been a slight, wiry fellow, with prominent cheekbones and long, stringy hair. Before him lay the bodies of two burly blokes, shaven-headed and at least ten years too old – as far as Kipper could judge. The men looked like they had been set on fire and buried.

"Well?" Bigby pressed for an answer although the smirk on his face suggested he already had one.

"Neither of them," Kipper's shoulders slumped.

"O-ho!" Bigby raised his voice. "So what you're telling me is that your friend Damien Deacus is not here?"

Kipper blushed and looked at his shoes.

"What's that, Inspector?" Bigby cupped his ear.

"No," Kipper muttered. "He ain't."

"So, is he dead or isn't he? According to you, he's buried in this very spot. Might he still be numbered among the living after all? Might he still be at large?"

Kipper shrugged. "I suppose."

"You suppose!" Bigby laughed. "I don't know what you boys are playing at down at Bow Street but if you can't tell whether a villain is dead or alive – well!"

Kipper shook his head. He could not look Bigby in the eye.

"Right," Bigby addressed the team. "Let's get these two back to the Yard and have a proper look at them. Find out who they are and what did them in."

The men began to wrap the bodies in the tarps and to gather up their equipment. Kipper did not move.

"You may come with us, you know," Bigby offered, gesturing to the police carriage into which everything had been loaded. "You never know; you might learn something."

***

Kipper would never say it out loud but he was impressed with the facilities at Scotland Yard. There was a special room for the examination of bodies, with white tiles on the floor and up the walls, and a pair of porcelain-topped tables with guttering. To drain away the fluids, he realised and shuddered.

The men from the grave were laid out on these tables and divested of their garments by the aid of a large pair of scissors. The clothes were handed to one of Bigby's team who began a systematic search of the pockets.

Meanwhile, Bigby introduced a fellow in a white coat and oilskin apron. "This is Chivers, our mortician. He'll have these chaps open and revealing their secrets faster than Father can carve the Christmas goose, what!"

Chivers nodded to Kipper. Kipper smiled weakly; he would much rather watch that fellow going through the effects of the deceased. He took the smirk on Bigby's face as an affront to his manliness and resolved not to allow his squeamishness to show.

"Right-o, Chivers. Let's see if we can find the sixpence, what!"

The mortician began with an inspection of the bodies, making marks on charts that bore outlines of the human form. He spoke his observations aloud. Kipper kept a smile on his face and nodded along, before deciding that a smile was not perhaps the appropriate expression in the presence of dead men and opted instead for a look of mild interest and respect.

"Both men appear to be middle-aged. Forties. No obvious signs of trauma. Burns to the head, neck and hands appear superficial."

"So they did not burn to death?" Bigby prompted.

"No, chief," said Chivers.

"Then why the fire? Killer trying to destroy evidence, do you think?"

"Doubt it," Chivers pursed his lips. "Not if he was going to bury them in any case."

"Sir?" A man came in, whom Kipper recognised from the graveyard. A couple of the team had been left to continue the excavation.

"Jim?" said Bigby. "What news?"

"We found a lantern. In the grave," Jim was breathless with excitement rather than from exertion.

"Oh?" said Bigby, teeth champing on his pipe. He turned to Kipper. "Thoughts, Inspector?"

"Um," said Kipper, taking a while to realise he was the inspector being addressed. "Well, it's obvious, ain't it? They had a lantern on account of it being dark, on account of it being night and all. See?"

Bigby's eyebrows went up. He turned back to Jim.

"Oil lamp, was it?"

"Sir, yes, sir."

"Could that account for the burns, then, Chivers?"

"I'd say so. If somebody chucked it at them."

Bigby sucked on his pipe as he considered this. "The question is who and why?" He turned to the man going through the clothes. "Any joy, Bob?"

Bob, a fellow who was also equipped with a pipe, approached with his hands full. He held out a battered wallet, a penknife, a soiled handkerchief and a length of string.

"Anything with any names on?" Bigby didn't sound hopeful.

"No, chief." He opened the wallet and tipped it over. A button fell out.

"Didn't think so. Chivers, before you do the honours, might I be a spoilsport and get my men to take prints from these gentlemen?"

Chivers bowed and stepped aside. He polished a couple of his enormous knives while he waited.

"Fingerprints—" Bigby began, but Kipper cut him off.

"Latest tool in the fight against crime," Kipper said. "I know."

He watched as a couple of men – how many were in Bigby's team? – went from hand to hand of the dead pair, pressing fingers carefully onto an ink pad and then rolling the fingertips onto a sheet of card with boxes drawn on for each digit.

"We'll see if these match anyone we know," said Bigby. "These chaps might have form."

Kipper nodded.

The fingerprint men scurried away to check the records. Chivers stretched like an athlete and stood over the first corpse.

"No obvious trauma," he repeated. "Going to start from the top down." He placed gloved hands on the dead man's head and turned it from side to side. "No contusions or abrasions," he intoned. "He wasn't struck on the bonce."

Bigby nodded, so Kipper nodded too.

"Hang about," Chivers's brow furrowed as his fingers moved down to the neck. "Something here."

"O-ho!" Bigby enthused. Kipper didn't know what to do.

Chivers reached for a magnifying glass and a pair of tweezers from his trolley. With a look of concentration, he worked away at the neck before pulling out a small, sharp point.

"O-ho!" said Bigby.

"A-ha?" said Kipper.

"Object appears to be a needle of some kind," Chivers held out the object.

"Interesting…" said Bigby. "Inspector?"

Damn it, thought Kipper. Why is he always picking on me, like an inattentive schoolboy?

"Sewing accident?" he offered.

"Oh! Good one!" Bigby guffawed a little too enthusiastically. "Chivers?"

"More like a dart, now that I look at it."

"What say you, Inspector? Pub tournament got out of hand?"

Kipper grunted. He wasn't prepared to commit to anything.

"Not pub dart. Poison dart, I reckon," Chivers continued. "They do this kind of thing abroad, sir. Cowardly way to do someone in, in my view. Quick puff of a pipe."

"Ugh," Bigby reflected. He removed his own pipe from his mouth and peered at it.

"Where?" said Kipper. "Where do they do this kind of thing?"

Chivers grimaced. "South America. Africa. Far East. You name it."

"China?"

"Yes, mate?"

"No. I mean, do they use such things in China?"

"Wouldn't be surprised."

Bigby looked at Kipper with renewed interest. "What's this, old man? Got a whiff of something in the old hooter, have we?"

"I don't know," said Kipper. "Just a thought… What about the other man?"

Chivers inspected the second man's neck and discovered an identical dart in a similar place. "I'll run a few tests on these little beauties. Might be traces of toxins on them."

"So…" Bigby proceeded to pace around. "Let's review. Two men in a grave that was not meant for them. The intended occupant is conspicuous by his absence and these two are slightly burned and it looks like poisoned with darts of unknown origin."

"That's about the size of it, chief," Chivers agreed. "I'll be able to tell more once I get them open. See the effects of the toxins."

He wielded his largest blade. Kipper stepped forward.

"Couldn't the dirt have killed them?" he said quickly. "You know, being buried alive, or the weight of it or something?"

"Unlikely," said Chivers. "Poison was most likely instantaneous. They dropped dead where they stood."

"And then they were covered over in the grave," Bigby nodded. "Seems straightforward to me. Proceed, man."

Chivers raised the blade but before he could bring it down again, his examination was interrupted by the sound of Inspector Kipper hitting the floor, having fainted clean away.

***

He came to in an office with a coat draped over him and his feet on a chair. Bigby was standing over him, puffing his pipe with a look of bemused concern.

"Back with us, old boy!" he observed. "Good man."

Kipper rubbed his eye with the heel of his hand and looked around. "What happened?"

Bigby smirked. "You hit the deck like an old lady in a heavy frost. Missed the lot. Old Chivers had those blokes in pieces almost as quickly. It's confirmed: death by poison. And, furthermore, my lads have uncovered the identity of our mystery men."

"Go on!" Kipper urged, keen to learn and keener still to get things wrapped up so he could get back to Bow Street.

"Turns out they're a pair of professional grave-robbers. Body-snatchers in the pay of most of the medicos in this city. Whoever did them in did us a favour. Saved us the job of tracking them down and subjecting them to due process of the law."

"Stroke of luck, then."

"But we can't have people going around bumping off body-snatchers left, right and centre. Makes us look bad."

But Kipper wasn't listening. He removed the coat and got to his feet. He paced while he thought and thought while he paced. "Hold on…"

"Johnny?" Bigby watched the inspector do a few laps of the room. "You're on the scent of something."

"I bloody am!" said Kipper. "Think about it: those two – why would they be in a grave?"

"Well, somebody did them in and hid the evidence."

"There's more to it than that."

"Go on."

"What if… What if they was there, plying their trade? They digs up the body – Damien Deacus's body, lest we forget – but somebody else wants it more than they do. Surprises them with a lamp and then, two quick darts to the neck and bosher!"

Bigby looked impressed. "You might not be as thick as you look, old man. Someone robbed the robbers!"

"Or…" Kipper was on a roll, "Somebody hired them to do the dirty work, dig up Deacus, and then silenced them so they couldn't rattle their chops."

"By Jove…" Bigby gaped in admiration. "The question remains: Who?"

"That's exactly right," said Kipper. "Hoo done it. I'd stake my orchestras on it."

***

He hurried back to Bow Street, worried that he had said too much. He didn't want Bigby and his great bunch of bastards to find Doctor Hoo before he did. Deep down, Kipper knew what was important was that the man be found, not who did the finding. But to him it was a matter of personal pride. He wanted to get one up on Scotland Yard and put a dent in the smug smiles of Bigby and his lads.

"Hello, sir!" Adams seemed surprised. "Wasn't expecting you until the morning."

"Doctor Hoo!" Kipper snapped, omitting the social niceties. "Where can I find him?"

"Well," Adams stroked his beard, "he's got a place on Harley Street. But you know that already."

"And the place is abandoned," Kipper added. "I need to find him and I need to find him pretty damn sharpish." He gave Adams a hopeful expression but the ever-resourceful sergeant could only shake his head.

"I haven't the foggiest, sir," he said sadly. "Wouldn't know where to begin."

"Oh, really, Adams?"

"I have been reading up, sir. Just in case you arsked me. Nobody don't know nothing about him, sir. Hasn't been heard of for donkeys'. Not since a bit of a how-d-you-do at the Lord Mayor's dinner, a few years back."

"Oh?" Kipper was intrigued.

"I dug about in the library, sir. Old newspapers. The dinner was ruined, sir. They all come home early, thanks to the..." He peered at his notepad, "...outrageous claims made by one of their profession."

"Claims, Adams?"

"Something about bringing new life... I didn't fully understand it, sir. I ain't no scientist... Transplants was mentioned. Reanimation."

"Oh..." Kipper peered at Adams's scrawled notes. "And you found this in the library, you say?"

"Matter of public record, sir."

"Good man!" he clapped the sergeant on the shoulder blade. "Keep digging. I want a list of all those who attended that dinner and interviews with the lot. Find out what they remember."

"Yes, sir!"

"That's going to take some time. I could do with finding this doctor as soon as possible."

"I only wish I could help, sir." Adams looked downcast.

"You already have, man."

He brought Adams up to speed with the latest from Scotland Yard. Adams listened, agog and wincing at the appropriate points in the account.

"Seems to me, sir," he scratched his hairy face, "the last people to see this Doctor Hoo was them poor buggers what was dug up."

"Yes..."

"But where did he meet them, sir? Where do you go to engage yourself a couple of body-snatchers?"

"Where indeed?"

"Star and Ferret, sir."

"I beg your pardon."

"It's a pub, sir. Down Cheapside way. There you can find all manner of neerdowells, sir. The bleedin' dregs of humanity. There you can find anybody to do anything you can think of, sir."

"Oh, really? And how do you know this, Sergeant?"

Adams bristled with pride as well as follicles. "Place is also riddled with our informants, sir. I take it you'll be going there, sir. Arsk for a glass collector by the name of Sprite, sir."

Inspector Kipper gaped.

"Little tyke, about yea high," Adams held out his hand.

"I know him!"

"Him, sir? I could have sworn he was a she."

"Really?"

"Well, if you knows him and you says he's a he, then who am I to argue with an inspector?"

"Cheapside, you said?"

"That's right, sir. Star and Ferret. The kind of place where you wipes your feet on the way out. I could come with you, sir."

"I don't want to be conspicuous."

"Out of me uniform, of course, sir."

"No, no; I'll be all right on me Molly Malone."

"If you're sure, sir. I'll get you a cab."

Adams left Kipper alone. The inspector fastened his coat and wrapped his muffler around his throat. He felt in his pockets. He had some loose change but not much. He would just have to hope that Sprite would price his information on the cheap side.

Thirteen

My head was still drowsy from Hoo's drugs but I staggered across the lab and tried the door, knowing full well it would still be locked. I was losing track of how long I'd been there. And I still couldn't fathom why Hoo was keeping me incarcerated like a common criminal. Why did he save me from the noose and rescue me from the grave if he's only going to keep me under lock and key?

Oh, yeah: on account of me trying to diddle him out of the toff's money.

But why give me new arms and not the liberty to enjoy them?

I was going to have it out with good old Doctor Hoo as soon as I set eyes on him. I just hoped he'd hurry up because I was getting rather hungry by this point. I paced around the lab like a caged animal in a forgotten zoo.

I tried to run my hand across my brow and almost broke me own nose. I wasn't used to my new hands; they was bigger and heavier than my old ones and the arms was a bit longer so I was having trouble judging distance with them. And talk about clumsy! I was flailing about like a broken windmill until I learned how to control them. Well, it looked like I had plenty of time to practise, didn't it? So I sat down and began with simple stuff, like counting on my fingers, one, two, three – well, you know how it goes. When I got to four, I had trouble with me ring finger; I couldn't shift it at all at first. I didn't half sweat and when I tried to wipe the sweat away I clobbered myself in the hooter again, because I done it without thinking.

After that, I tried to button my shirt. It was like trying to knit with sausages instead of needles. Hours I must have spent but I was determined to master it. After all, a man must be able to dress himself. Even if he has a butler, like that toff.

Speaking of that toff, I wondered how he was getting on. Edward, Lord Beighton. How was he getting on with one leg? At least my arms was a matching pair. My guess was he was limping around, dragging his new foot behind him. Probably claiming it as a war wound or hunting injury or something. The posh git.

But who cares about him? I had problems of my own. I got me arms behaving themselves but it was my belly's turn for rebellion. My Auntie Nelly was gurgling and rumbling, trying to get my attention. Feed me, it was saying, as if I didn't know I was hungry.

I went to the door again and, slowly, closed my hand around the door knob. I turned it, pleased with the way my fingers was almost behaving normally. But the door was still locked. I was stuck like a cocked hat in a trap. Even the thought of a cocked hat – or 'rat' if you ain't a Cockney – was beginning to have its appeal. Why, if one crept across the laboratory floor that minute, I wouldn't have fancied its chances of reaching the other side.

When I was in prison, I heard stories of men what had supplemented their diet of gruel and stale bread with the occasional rodent what they had caught. I never did. But then, I didn't have to. I was under sentence of death so I was rather well looked after, all things considered. Odd, ain't it? You're the worst of the worst and your days is numbered but the prison does its best to make you comfortable – within reason, of course. I had a cell to myself. My own personal guards to chat to. Regular visits from the chaplain. And the food – well! I'd never eaten so well in all my born days. "Got to keep your strength up," my mates, the guards, kept joking. They was decent types. And I reckon they was relieved I didn't try to take them down with me. They told me all sorts of tales about murderers who had tried their luck one last time, railing against the system and doing in a guard or two, for good measure. And there was others, hardened criminals who could make you shit yourself just by looking at you, breaking down into tears and crying for their mothers. Not me. Well, I never had no mother to cry out for, for one thing, but I was calm and collected, like I was waiting for an omnibus, they said. Like I was going on a bleedin' holiday not to meet my maker or his horned subordinate.

I think it was because I knew Hoo wouldn't let me down. I knew he'd get me out. And then the night before the rope was due to go around my bushel and peck, he turned up. Said something about examining me to see if I was fit to stand execution. Well, they fell for it, hook, line and bleedin' sinker – or perhaps they decided it wasn't worth arguing with him on account of him not speaking English as good as what we does. Hoo slipped me a little packet, a roll of paper with powder in it. He signalled that I was to take it with a drink of water and so I did. Then he goes and before long I'm foaming at the mouth and cramped up in terrible bleedin' agony and the men calls him back and he says I must go to hospital right away, and they bundles me in the back of a wagon and I'm sinking fast and starting to think getting me neck stretched would be better than being poisoned to death. Everything goes grey and then black and then there's nothing. I hear Hoo's voice, all faint like he's a long way orf, telling them I'm brown bread, only he don't use them words exactly – he might not say much but he's well-spoken is Doctor Hoo. Next thing I knows, I'm waking up in that coffin – but you knows about that bit already.

And now he's got me locked up in here, without so much as a rat to keep me going.

I'd said I was sorry. For switching the money bags. I don't know what else I could have done.

I lay down and stewed with only the rumblings of my Auntie Nelly for company. I almost wished that toff would come back so I could have run rings around him, intellectually speaking. And I was just dozing off when I heard the warehouse door slide open and shut. Either that or it was a giant yawning. I froze, and held me breath. I couldn't hear nothing so I knew it was Hoo all right, on account of his ability to shift himself without making a sound – unless he wanted to. I thought about making a racket to remind him of his forgotten prisoner and clatter and bang about the place until I drove him to distraction. But then I stopped myself. I went off that idea sharpish. What if it weren't Hoo but some other dangerous eccentric? At least I was safely locked in. And if he tried to bash the door in, well, I'd be ready, wouldn't I, to do the same to his brains because nobody can break through a locked door and be silent about it, can they? I'd be ready as soon as I heard him. Even my clumsy new chalks could do some damage if I swung 'em about hard enough.

"Awake?"

It was Doctor Hoo, standing behind me and I hadn't heard a peep. I spun around and was about to suggest he take up house-breaking or assassinating or something, when I saw what he was holding, or rather smelled it. He was holding a tea tray with a bowl of golden noodle soup on it. My stomach pulled me toward it like a puppy on its leash, eager for walkies.

"That for me, is it?" I tried to appear casual and collected.

Hoo shook his head – barely. "Queen Mother," he said. He put the tray on the bench and backed away with a little bow. I didn't need telling twice.

I sat on the bench and reached for the bowl. "Hoi! What's this?" He'd only bleedin' gone and brought me chopsticks! For soup! Another of his little jokes. He *was* in a good mood and no mistake.

I cupped my hands around the bowl – slow and careful; I didn't want to spill any of it. I lifted it to my mouth, aware that the doctor's minces were on me. Puckering my lips, I tilted the bowl, sending soup splashing down me front.

Hoo nodded. "Practise," he advised.

"What do you think I've been doing in here, while you've had me banged up like a common criminal?"

"Eat," was his next piece of advice. And he was right and all; I didn't want the soup to get cold. My second attempt was more successful. I drank the clear, golden liquid, feeling the spices warm me insides and I slurped at the noodles like the earliest bird getting all the bleedin' worms.

When I'd finished I wiped the back of my hand across my north and south, taking care not to give myself a thick lip in the process. I was feeling a lot better and more disposed to having a proper chinwag with the doctor rather than knocking his block off.

"Why did you do this to me, Doctor?" I asked his immovable mask of a face. "Why'd you give me these?" I hunched my shoulders. The brass fittings rose and fell under my shirt.

Hoo lifted a finger to quiet me. He seemed on the verge of saying something when we was both surprised by loud and repeated banging from downstairs. Somebody was hammering on the door like they meant it. A glance passed between me and Hoo.

"I don't think that's a giant bleedin' woodpecker, do you?"

"Unlikely," he replied. "Stay."

He glided from the laboratory and closed the door behind him. I tiptoed over to it and listened my hardest.

The banging stopped. I heard the door slide open and voices.

It was the police!

Fourteen

Kipper heard the pub before he saw it; its general din of loud conversation, raucous singing and demonic laughter greeted him as he skirted the corner of Watling Street – and the pub was at the other end! He made his way toward the comparatively inviting glow of its windows, like a moth desperate for hard liquor. The street was dark, devoid of lampposts and Kipper paid heed to what he might be treading in. At least there's no fog, he reflected.

There was fog though, only it was inside the Star and Ferret. A dense pall of tobacco smoke hung in the air like a cloud that had popped in for a swift half and had ended up making a night of it. Kipper stood on the threshold, spotted the location of the bar and made his way through the melee. The tapster, he hoped, would know the whereabouts of the diminutive glass collector and might even disclose them for only a modest gratuity.

"Here!" a burly bloke in Kipper's path spun around and glared at him. "You lookin' at my pint?"

Kipper was flummoxed. "I – I – I," he stammered, his voice seizing up when he was faced with the bloke's broad and hairy fist.

"You better buy him another one," advised a rat-faced ruffian at the burly bloke's elbow. "And me and all."

"I don't want no trouble," said Kipper. He reached inside his coat. Burly and Ratface sneered – but they were sneers of encouragement. Surely, fresh pints of ale could not be far away. Their faces swiftly changed when they were presented, not with a pound note but a police officer's warrant card.

They scarpered. In an instant, unspoken word got around the pub and within seconds it was empty. Even the cloud did a runner. As the door clattered shut behind the last to leave, Kipper approached the bar, trying to ignore the squelches of his shoes on the sawdust.

The tapster was glaring at him with eyes like hot coals. He did not even glance at the warrant card. "We don't serve your kind in here," he growled.

"Good," said Kipper. "I'm not here to buy one. I'm after Sprite."

The barman gave a one-shouldered shrug. Kipper blinked twice.

"Looks like I'll have to settle in for the evening. I can't imagine how that'll affect your takings."

He cast around as though selecting the best place to sit.

The barman grunted. His fingers itched to fetch his trusty cricket bat from under the counter.

"It's all right, Bert," said a voice behind Kipper's back. "I know him, I do."

Kipper turned to see the urchin, a little cleaner than the last time – at least, the hands. From washing glasses, he supposed. The face too had recently been in contact with water, however fleetingly. Cheeks, nose and forehead had a pinkish hue but the child's neck was still as black as soot.

"Hello, Inspector," Sprite smirked. "'Ow may I be of hassistance?"

Kipper looked over his shoulder at Bert the barman, who threw up his hands in despair.

"Take it outside, if you please," he groaned. "Perhaps some of me customers'll come back in."

"Through here," said Sprite, leading Kipper to a side door.

Out in an alley, Sprite assured him they would not be disturbed. "The dollymops don't tend to use this place," Sprite took on the air of a tour guide, "on account of too many of their punters' wives drinking in the same boozer."

The urchin waited with a patient smile. Kipper gave up trying to divine the child's gender and got down to business.

"That place... In Harley Street..."

"I never took nothing!" Sprite was quick to interrupt.

"I'm not saying you did. Whose place is it?"

"That's right," said Sprite.

"What?"

"It's Hoo's place, all right. Only he ain't been there for donkeys'. You saw the state of it, Inspector. Like a desert with windows."

"And you have no idea where he might be found?"

"Who?"

"That's right."

Sprite's head shook slowly. "You don't want to be messing with the likes of him, Inspector."

"I don't want to mess with him. I only want to arsk him a few questions."

"Well," Sprite's hand rubbed the back of Sprite's neck and came away filthy.

"If it's a question of..." Kipper produced a sixpence. Sprite snatched it away, quick as a wink.

"It ain't that..." the urchin shrugged. "It's just that I don't want you getting hurt."

"I'm touched," said Kipper, furnishing another coin.

"You'd have to be," said Sprite, whisking the second tanner away.

"Putting your concern for my welfare aside for a moment, do you or don't you know the whereabouts of this Doctor Hoo?"

"Oh, I knows all right. There ain't much goes on in this town that don't come to my attention sooner or later."

A third coin exchanged hands.

"Well?"

"Well what?"

"Are you going to tell me?"

"No, mate," Sprite grinned. "I can do better than that. I'm going to take you there myself."

***

Kipper allowed himself to be led by the urchin with something approaching utmost trust. There was something about the urchin that inspired his faith: if Sprite said it then it was undoubtedly true. It went against Kipper's instincts as a copper but he didn't seem to mind that either – Oh, I ain't stupid, he reminded himself. I'm well aware this little bastard could be leading me up the garden path – and by garden path, I mean a dark alley where a bunch of confederates lie in wait to ambush me with the hiding of my life. Kipper thumbed the cosh in his overcoat pocket: If I'm going down, I'm cracking a few loaves open on my way.

Not that he truly believed that for a second that the dirty urchin was leading him to his doom. Head held high, Sprite strode through the streets of London as if he (or she) was the landlord (landlady). They encountered no one on their route to the docks at Limehouse, even though the clangour of activity on the river was growing louder with every step they took. Even at night, the waterside was busy, with cargoes being loaded or unloaded – Kipper was willing to bet most of it was far from legit but that was not the reason he was there. He trailed after Sprite across the waterfront to where hulking shapes loomed ahead, darker shadows against the night sky.

"This is the one," Sprite came to a stop, punctuating the announcement with a wet sniff. "Hoo's new gaff."

Kipper looked the edifice up and down; it seemed exactly like all the others. "What makes you so sure?"

Sprite winked and clicked his teeth. Or her teeth – oh, this is maddening, thought Kipper! I must ask! Are you Abel or Mabel?

"Like I said, there ain't nothing that don't come to my attention sooner or later. Ain't you going to knock?"

"What?"

"Only I find it the most expeditious way of letting 'em know you're here."

"I know what knocking is, thank you. Here." He handed the child a shilling. Sprite pocketed it but did not move.

"Ain't you got nowhere to go?" Kipper scowled. "Only I'm running out of cash."

"Oh, no, mate," Sprite grinned. "I ain't going nowhere. I'm going to help out, ain't I?"

"Oh, no, mate," Kipper bristled. "I can't allow that. This is police business. You might get hurt."

"So might you," the urchin observed.

"That's what they pays me for."

"No, it ain't. They pays you to catch the criminals. Listen to me a minute, Inspector. While you knock on the door and do things up front and proper, like, I'll have a squint around the back."

"No; I can't allow it."

"Tough biscuits; it's happening."

With that, Sprite knocked on the warehouse door and sped around the corner, leaving a nonplussed and befuddled inspector dithering at the doorway.

I could murder that little—

Kipper's homicidal thoughts were cut short as the wide warehouse door slid aside to reveal a tall, gaunt figure cast into silhouette by the lamplight behind him.

"Um – er..." Kipper fumbled his warrant card from his pocket. "Doctor Hoo."

"It says 'Kipper,'" intoned the slender figure. "*I* am Hoo."

He stepped back and made a sparse gesture, an invitation to enter. Kipper swallowed; it was peculiar but with Sprite no longer at close quarters, the inspector was experiencing the choking grip of fear. He entered the warehouse, like a storage place for shadows, and heard the door slide shut behind him.

"This way," his host's voice rumbled. Hoo picked up the lamp and his face sprang into view; Kipper let out an involuntary gasp.

It's only a mask, only a mask, only a mask – he told himself but then the way the cheek curled as the slightest of smiles teased the edge of Hoo's thin lips told the inspector this was no mask.

He bleedin' looks like that! Stone me! What have you got yourself into, Johnny?

As they crossed the warehouse floor, Kipper saw the doctor's shadow stretch up the wall, eldritch and otherworldly, like something from a Germanic fairy story. They came to a pair of wooden chairs. Hoo stooped and set the lantern on the floor between them before inviting the inspector to sit. When his guest was settled, Hoo folded himself onto the chair opposite. Lit from below, the mask-like features looked more than ever like they had been carved from wood.

A silent moment elapsed.

"Tea?" said Doctor Hoo.

"Oh, gawd, no!" cried Inspector Kipper, a little louder and quicker than he would have liked. "I mean, no, thank you, but no."

He blushed. The lamplight danced in the doctor's narrow eyes. Hoo was amused by the policeman's discomfort.

"Questions?" the lips parted and the thin moustaches drooped like untied bootlaces.

"Oh? Oh, yes. Yes. I've got questions all right." Kipper took a look at his notebook; it was a prop, merely – he knew exactly what he wanted to ask. "Fellow by the name of…" Quick glance at a random entry. "Deacus. Damien Deacus. Did you know him, Doctor?"

Hoo's eyes locked on the inspector's, his expression inscrutable.

"Well?" Kipper prompted.

"Yes," Hoo's head inclined but slightly yet the shadows swam under his sharp features.

"In what capacity?"

"He *worked* for me."

The intonation was peculiar; Kipper couldn't fathom what it might signify. He pretended to make a mark in his book.

"Go to his funeral, did you?"

Hoo did not respond. Kipper made another note with an extravagant flourish of his pencil.

"Or did you show up afterwards? Did you turn up when it was all over with two blokes and a couple of shovels and dig up his body? By any chance?"

Hoo made a sound at the back of his throat to indicate he found the inspector's questions mildly amusing.

"Where's the body, Doctor? Where's Damien Deacus?"

Hoo rose, towering over the inspector. Kipper shrank back. Hoo smiled and gestured broadly to a spiral staircase in a corner.

"He is here," he said.

Fifteen

The bastard! The bloody bastard! He's only bleedin' turnin' me in! After everything I've done for him and all!

The bloody bleedin' bloody bastard!

Panic gripped me and I jumped up and down a bit on the spot. I had to get out of there and run for my bleedin' life.

There was a window, a small square high up, grey with grime. That would have to do. I shoved the table over to it and climbed up, bringing a chair with me for additional height. My new, longer arms could just about reach the latch but my new, thicker fingers wouldn't quite bend as I needed them to.

I could hear them coming up the stairs – well, not the doctor, obviously, because he don't make a sound in them flat, black slippers he wears, but I could hear the copper's hobnail boots all right. Time was running out. I didn't want to go back to prison – who would? And, call me peculiar, I certainly didn't want to get sentenced to hang all over again. I'd escaped the noose once and I didn't want to push my luck.

At last, the latch did what it was told and I pushed the little window open. It creaked in protest. I jumped up and grabbed the sill with my clumsy new hands and got the fright of my life.

A face was staring in at me. Right at me. A pair of bright eyes in a pink face that was smeared with black – or it might have been a black face blotted with pink – I didn't get the chance to have a good look at it, on account of when it said 'Boo!' in a high-pitched voice like a kid's, I was so startled I sprang backwards, lost my grip on the windowsill and fell off the chair – and the table and all. I landed on my Aristotle just as the door opened and in came the doctor, ushering his guest to step inside.

The double-crossing, treacherous…

"This is him, is it?" said the copper with a sniff. "Only to my untrained eye he don't look all that dead."

He approached but didn't offer to help me up. He treated me to a swift squint at his warrant card.

"Damien Deacus?" he asked.

"No, mate," I did my best to look sorry for disappointing him. "You just missed him." I pointed at the window, which was ajar. The copper looked sceptical and turned to that traitor Doctor Hoo.

"It is he," said the doctor, calm as anything. I thought about chucking the chair at him.

Apparently, his word was good enough for the copper, who pulled out a set of handcuffs and announced he was arresting me.

"What for?" Well, I had a right to know. I glared at the doctor but it was like trying to faze a cucumber. Surely Hoo hadn't turned me in just because I tried to diddle him out of that toff's money.

"Suspicion of murder," the copper said grimly, and that stopped me in my tracks, I can tell you. Somewhat dazed, I stood there blinking like a cow with concussion as the copper pulled my hands behind my back and clicked the cuffs around my wrists.

"Murder?" Even saying the word out loud didn't make it any more believable. I may be a lot of things but I ain't never killed nobody in all my struggle and strife (not on purpose, any road) – although at that moment I would have had a bloody good go at polishing off Doctor bleedin' Hoo if I had my brass bands free.

"Three murders," said the copper. "But you can tell us all about them down at Bow Street nick."

He bundled me toward the door.

"Here! What is this?" I tried to dig my heels in but the copper kept shoving. "Tell him! Doctor! I ain't no murderer!"

Hoo's face was a graven image. If anything, he looked a little bit bored by this disruption to his evening.

"Who am I supposed to have murdered then, eh?" I tried to wedge myself in the doorway. "Tell me that."

"Ignorance is no defence," said the copper. "I've got you bang to rights, Damien Deacus, or should I say, 'Foggy Jack'?"

It was like a punch in the kisser. And then I laughed. "What's this? You're having a giraffe! You think that I'm – Oh, tell him, Doctor!"

But Hoo wasn't even looking at me. After that, it was easy for the copper to steer me down the stairs. By the time he got me outside into the damp and chilly air, I was ready to chuck myself into the bleedin' river.

A police wagon was waiting and a copper in uniform saluted as we approached. He had a bushy red beard like a squirrel's Aristotle had exploded on his face.

"Get him, sir?" said this copper from somewhere behind all that ginger fur.

"Sergeant Adams?" My copper seemed surprised to see him. "How did you—"

Sergeant Bushy-beard Adams tapped the side of his nose. "A little bird told me, sir. A little bird about yea high, covered in muck, sir."

This got similar reactions from my copper and me. We both seemed to know who he was talking about. That face at the window that had stopped me climbing out…

My eyes darted around the dock. I wouldn't have been surprised to see that filthy face leering at me from the shadows.

So that was two people whose scores I had to settle. The dirty-faced kid and the treacherous doctor. But what could I do? I supposed I'd have to come back and haunt the bastards. See how they like that.

***

How bloody lovely to be back at Bow Street nick! I'm being sarcastic, of course. I was searched – I don't know what they was expecting to find. A big knife and a signed confession, perhaps. Yes, I am Foggy Jack all right and you've got me bang to rights. Huh! They should be so bleedin' lucky.

They shoved me into a room and said they was going to take my fingerprints. Have 'em, I said, I ain't using them. Nobody laughed. Can't say I blame them.

This was where I ran into a spot of bother. They told me to roll my fingers across an inkpad and then press them onto a sheet of paper. Well, it sounds simple enough, don't it? Only my new chalks had other ideas. I could hardly lift them and the effort made me break out in a sweat, adding to my general air of looking guilty, I shouldn't be surprised. Perhaps it was being shoved and pulled around, or perhaps it was falling off that table what done it but I reckon my brass fittings needed tightening or loosening or something.

Anyway, I managed to lift my arms enough to flop them on the table. The inspector – Kipper his name was – took to swearing under his breath. In the end, he took my hand and he rolled my fingers one by one over the inkpad.

"Being stubborn won't help you," he said, between the swears.

"I'm not being," I said, but he wasn't having none of it.

"How long have you been an opium addict?" he asked all of a sudden.

"You what?"

"Is that what's making your arms all floppy? Or is it the chronic self-abuse?"

"I beg yours!"

"Is that what's making you do all them horrible murders? The opium. Proper little fiend, ain't you?"

Well, I didn't know which question to answer first.

"Self-abuse?" I scoffed. "I can honestly say these hands have never taken advantage of my body."

"And the murders? Have these hands murdered three women?"

Well, I couldn't know that, could I? They could have been up to all sorts before I got them.

"Not as long as I've had them, no."

The piece of paper was full of black smudges. Kipper handed it to that bearded bastard, who hurried out of the room with it like it was an urgent despatch from the bleedin' Queen.

"Now," says Kipper, taking a seat across the table from me, "while we're waiting for your prints to be checked, let's have a bit of a natter, shall we?"

I looked around for something to wipe my inky fingers on.

"You are Damien Deacus," he said. What a waste of time and breath that was!

"I ain't never said I wasn't," I replied.

"And you're also the murderer of three women."

"Piss off."

"Let's not forget our manners, Mr Deacus."

"Please piss off."

"All right then. First things first. You was pronounced dead the night before you was due to be hanged by your scrawny neck. Then you was buried but you are now, alive and kicking."

I hadn't kicked nobody yet but I was willing to start with him.

"Care to explain?"

"Well… I couldn't have been dead, could I? Buried alive, I was. Oh, it was horrible."

"But you got out."

"Yeah. Evidently."

"How?"

"Well…" I stopped to think. There was no way I was going to grass up Doctor Hoo even though he practically served me up on a plate; I know how to be loyal even if he don't. "Lucky them grave robbers come along, weren't it?"

"Ah, yes," Kipper nodded. "Two grave robbers who ended up

dead and buried in your grave."

I tried to shrug but my brass fittings seized up. My shoulders went up but didn't come down again. Inspector Kipper clocked all this and looked at me like I was odd.

"There was a scuffle," I said, "a right old kerfuffle. I just got out of there fast as I could. You can understand that; I'd had an 'orrible experience. What happened after me back was turned, well, how am I supposed to know that?"

Kipper pouted. He wasn't having none of that neither.

"So you didn't shoot those men with poison darts?"

"Me, Inspector? No. Cross my heart." I tried to but only succeeded in making my hands flop about a bit.

"Somebody shot those men with poison darts."

"Somebody else. Look, I don't know much about grave robbing nor nothing like that but I shouldn't be surprised if it weren't a rival gang or something what done them in. Stands to reason."

He thought about it. He didn't like it but I could see he found it plausible. One up to me!

"All right," he says. "Let's put your miraculous resurrection to one side for a minute. We've got your fingerprints at the scenes of numerous crimes in Harley Street, to wit: the thefts of various medical instruments, the likes of which have been used in the murders of three prostitutes in recent weeks."

"Oh, have you, now?"

"Yes, we have. Come off it, Mr Deacus. You're our man, ain't you? You're our killer."

Before I could curl my lip in the sneer of disdain his comments deserved, the door burst open and in came that sergeant, running in after his beard like a child eating candy floss.

"Sir, sir! It ain't him, it ain't him!" he pointed at me.

"I told you that," I said.

"What?" Kipper got up. The sergeant handed him the sheet of fingerprints.

"According to those we've got on file, which match those found at Harley Street, that man sitting there ain't Damien Deacus!"

"You what?" said the inspector and he stared at me.

And then it struck me, what Doctor Hoo had done. Not only had he given me new arms, he'd given me a new set of fingerprints and all. He'd swapped my arms not to punish me but to protect me! The clever old basket.

"Well," I says, managing to fold my arms – just about – "it couldn't have been me what nicked them medical things then, could it?"

I sat back while the inspector and the sergeant gaped at me all incredulous.

"So I can go now, can I?"

Kipper ran a hand down his face. He looked exhausted.

"No," said the sergeant, surprising me and the inspector both. "These prints belong to notorious safe-cracker and bank robber, Jedidiah Plank. We've been looking for you for ages."

"Ha!" said Kipper.

"Oh, bloody hell," said I.

***

They bunged me in a cell while they gathered a list of my crimes – not the crimes of Damien Deacus, oh no, (it would be a short bleedin' list) but the crimes of this Jedidiah Plank, whoever he may be – or rather, whoever he *was*, because I don't think Doctor Hoo took the arms off of a living bloke, do you? So, how did he come by them? Did he have this Plank geezer dug up? Or did he do away with him himself?

No.

Hard to imagine Doctor Hoo getting his gloves soiled doing his own dirty work.

The cell was small, little bigger than the bunk it contained. There was also a bucket – well, you can imagine what that was for; I hoped I wouldn't be in there long enough to need it.

I had to convince them I wasn't this Plank geezer – but how? Fingerprints don't lie; that Kipper took great pride in telling me. He was keen to see me go down for something. You could see it in his eyes. He knew he couldn't convict me for my own crimes, on account of I'd already been tried and sentenced for them, and you can't do a man twice for the same misdemeanour. It's the rules or something.

I tried pacing the cell as an aid to thinking but I may as well have spun pirouettes on the spot so I gave that up and stretched out on the bunk and held my hands where I could get a butcher's at them.

Oh, Doctor Hoo, I guess you meant well and was trying to save me from arrest. Perhaps you should have got me new chalks off of a vicar or somebody. Mind you, some of them vicars can get up to all sorts, can't they? You can't trust nobody these days.

I practised clenching my fists and turning my wrists. I bent my fingers one by one and everything was in working order. Perhaps I would get the hang of it – poor choice of words! Well, it depends on what this Plank had been up to. Somehow I didn't think I'd get away with a slap on the back of me legs. At least that Kipper bloke probably didn't think I was Foggy bleedin' Jack no more.

I put Plank's hands over my eyes and groaned and couldn't help wondering if I'd been better off back when I was buried alive.

Sixteen

Kipper didn't know what to think. He had been so sure he was on the right track. Damien Deacus had stolen all those medical instruments, which he had then used to commit three grisly murders – Kipper had checked the dates and none of the dollymops had met their gruesome fate while Deacus had been banged up, waiting to be hanged up.

That was another thing. The whole not-being-where-he-was-buried. And now, here he was, banged up again, only his fingerprints said the man in the cell wasn't Damien Deacus but some other villain. Kipper had sent Sergeant Adams to dig up Jedidiah Plank's file. Let's see what this toe rag has been up to; maybe I can fit the murders onto him.

Yes, I know it's only dollymops. Who gives a toss about dollymops? Well, it ain't them – it's their clientele. The toffs don't feel safe to walk the streets looking for streetwalkers. And we can't have that now, can we? Poor little toffs.

Nah, screw 'em. Kipper thumped his desk. The killer must be stopped no matter who his victims are.

And it would be better if I could be the one to stop him before any of those smug bastards down at Scotland Yard.

Sergeant Adams bustled in, his face ashen above his bright beard.

"There you are," said Kipper. "Did you bring that file?"

"Sir," Adams placed a bulging folder on the desk. "There's been another one."

"Another file?"

"Another murder, sir. Another dollymop. Down in Smithfield."

"Good gawd!" Kipper sprang to his feet. "And how do you know this?"

105

"One of the bobbies, sir."

"He found her, did he?"

"No, sir. He was nearly knocked over in the rush, sir."

"Rush? Damn it, Adams; stop speaking in riddles. What bleedin' rush?"

"Your colleagues, sir. From Scotland Yard. Falling over themselves, they was. Constable Harding just happened to be in the way."

"Damn it," Kipper thumped the desk again. "Where?"

"Smithfield, sir."

Kipper grabbed his hat.

"There's a cab waiting, sir."

***

The bleedin' bastards from Scotland Yard were all over the crime scene by the time Kipper arrived. The area – a corner of the market, an alley between halls – was secured with rope and bobbies standing guard. Kipper sought to get through the cordon but was intercepted by Bigby.

"Ah, there you are, old man!" He clapped an arm around Kipper's shoulder, champing enthusiastically on his pipe. "I knew you'd show up sooner or later."

Kipper stiffened. "Who is she?"

Bigby pulled a face. "Difficult to say at this juncture, old boy."

"Why?"

"Well…" Bigby grimaced. "The nature of her injuries – the extent of them – we're just about certain she was female."

Kipper frowned. "What do you mean?" He took a step toward the rope but Bigby pulled him back.

"I'd advise against it, Johnny. Going to be having nightmares for weeks myself."

Kipper extricated himself from Bigby's clutches and lifted the rope. A bobby bristled but a nod from Bigby stood him down.

"All right, Johnny," Bigby called after him. "Don't say I didn't warn you."

Kipper strode into the alley as keen to get away from that prick Bigby as he was to see the body. His foot splashed in a puddle and the thought flashed across his mind that there had been no rain that day. He looked at the toe of his boot. It shone, wet and red.

He trod more carefully.

At first he thought it was a pile of meat. Waste from the butchers' stalls, stacked up for disposal later. Perhaps the body was behind it. But as he drew nearer, he realised with a sick, sinking sensation in the pit of his stomach that this pink and glistening pyramid *was* the body, the mortal remains of some poor girl who had fallen foul of Foggy Jack.

He's made mincemeat of her!

Kipper's stomach rolled but he forced himself to look, despite gagging at the heady stench of blood and offal. A fly ambled nonchalantly down the slope of shredded flesh. Kipper retched and considered himself fortunate to have missed lunch that day. Breakfast too, come to think of it.

At the apex of the crude pyramid was a wig of blonde hair – No, Kipper realised! It was no wig. It was her scalp! At the base, a pair of boots and, at the sides, the woman's hands – the only parts of her to remain intact. Everything else was finely chopped and ground up as though it had been through a machine.

Pale and shining with a sheen of sweat, Kipper turned away from the hideous sight and returned to the rope.

"Told you so," Bigby greeted him but his tone was sombre. "Enough to put you off corned beef for life, what!"

Kipper gasped in lungfuls of the comparatively fresher air. "He – he butchered her."

"Good and proper," Bigby agreed. "At least we can take her fingerprints, poor cow. If she's been in bother before, we might be able to put a name to her."

Kipper's mind was racing. "Machinery," he said.

"What's that, old boy?"

"To do such a thorough job, he must have used a machine."

"My thoughts exactly," Bigby nodded. "My lads are asking around now. Which butchers use mincing apparatus and all that."

Damn it, thought Kipper. One step behind again.

***

Kipper absented himself from the removal of the remains, certain that he could add nothing to the proceedings other than vomit. Instead, he sought out the butcher he had spoken to previously. He found him tending his stall; his part of the market was all but deserted – everyone was swarming to get as close to the crime scene as possible. The butcher brightened a little when he recognised the copper and his eagerness to know more about what was going on sparkled in his eyes.

"Good day, Inspector!"

"Not for some," grumbled Kipper. He flashed his warrant card to indicate he was there in his official capacity.

"Bad business," the butcher shook his head.

"Bad *for* business too, I shouldn't wonder," Kipper shot back. "It's enough to make one turn vegetarian."

The butcher looked scandalised. "Wash your mouth out, Inspector!" He placed his hands over the ears of a pig's head on his display. He nodded back the way the copper had come. "Messy, was it?"

Kipper thought about it. That was the thing about these murders: they weren't messy. They were all arranged – *staged*, you might say, as though the killer was trying to get your attention and hold onto it. He shook his head.

"I'm not at liberty to disclose details of an ongoing investigation."

"Bloody hell," moaned the butcher.

"That is one way to describe it."

"But it was him, wasn't it?"

"Who?"

"Foggy Jack."

Kipper cringed and his eyes darted from side to side as though he feared the butcher might summon the devil. "Don't call him that! Like I said, I'm not at liberty to—"

"Yeah, yeah, and I said bloody hell."

Kipper took out his notepad but found he had nothing to write with. He patted his pockets. The butcher offered a stub of a pencil. It was sticky and slimy and a glob of gristle fell off it and blotted Kipper's page.

"Thanks," said Kipper, trying not to gag. "Now, what can you tell me about mincing?"

The butcher smirked. "Well, I reckon it's all about walking only on the balls of your feet. And the hips – they're very important – you moves 'em like this. And the hands go like this." He demonstrated by sashaying to and fro behind his stall. It took Kipper a while to realise the man was making a joke. The butcher's pursed lips could no longer contain his laughter.

"Your face, Inspector! Just pulling your pizzle. Trying to inject a bit of whatsit – levity into your day."

"I'd be obliged if you didn't waste my time."

The butcher's face fell. "You mean the mincing of meat; of course you do. You have to be careful with mincemeat, let me tell you." He lowered his voice. "There's plenty of unscrupulous traders round here who – well, let me just say it's not all exactly meat what goes through their mincers, if you catch my meaning."

Kipper had to confess he didn't.

"Well, it ain't just meat. It's bones and all. Fat. Gristle. Hooves. Eyeballs, liver, lights. The lot. Hair. All of it gets minced up together – makes the meat go further. Good business practice. In a sense. Not me, though, of course. You won't catch me stuffin' nothin' but the choicest cuts through my mincer; no, sir."

"Might I have a look at it?"

"Look at what?"

"Your equipment?"

"Ooh, Inspector. You're a fast one, ain't you? Ain't even bought me a drink yet."

Kipper glowered until the butcher's amusement ebbed.

"Sorry, Inspector. The wife thinks I'm a proper cut-up."

"I'm sure she does."

"D'you get it? A butcher who's a cut-up!"

"No," said Kipper. "Show me your mincer."

The butcher adopted a more serious attitude and pulled out a device from under the table. It was about ten inches tall and coated in white enamel. There was a handle on one side and a circular plate riddled with holes on the other. The top was an open maw revealing spiked rollers within.

"Here we go. You see, it's got a clamp on it here, what holds it to the table, so you've got both hands free, see? One hand to crank the handle and the other to feed meat into the top."

He demonstrated. Kipper saw the pair of rollers turn inside.

"Bit like a mangle, you see. The rollers pull the meat in and it gets shoved out through the holes there, see?"

"I see," said Kipper. "It's a bit small, ain't it?"

The butcher cupped his hands protectively around the machine.

"Must take a while…"

"It can be time-consuming, yes. That's why I only does it when people arsks for it. Then they see what they're getting. Not like other traders with their pre-minced minced meat. Could be anything in there and besides you don't know how long it's been sitting there, all congealin' and coagulatin' and flyblown… Here you ain't half gone pale, Inspector; are you all right?"

Kipper tried to nod. He was awash with sweat at the thought of those remains. Just sitting there, congealin' and coagulatin'. He remembered the fly… His legs buckled but he managed not to swoon. He held onto the edge of the table and found himself eye-to-eye with the pig's head. He sprang back, revolted.

Concern was etched on the butcher's features. "You look like you could do with a sit-down, Inspector. And some brandy."

Kipper struggled to compose himself. "What about…" he cleared his throat, "What if somebody was to order something big. Like a whole pig, say. And wanted it minced up."

The butcher rubbed his chin. "Unlikely. I'd advise against it. It'd take me too bleedin' long, for one thing. Have to cut it up, see. Debone and all. No, mate, you'd need a much bigger mincer than what I've got. Why'd you arsk? Police having a do, are they? Only you'd be better off keeping that pig whole and ramming a spit up its jacksy and roasting it over a fire. Lovely."

"No, no… And where might one find a larger mincer? In London, say?"

The butcher frowned. "Wouldn't have a clue, mate – Hold up! It *is* a clue, ain't it? Gawd above, are you saying he minced her? Foggy Jack minced her up?"

"Er – no!" Kipper was quick to interject. "I ain't saying that at all." He pocketed his notebook. "Thank you for your time."

He hurried away from the stall, cringing as the butcher's questions rang in his ears.

"He did, didn't he? He bloody did! Foggy Jack minced her up! Didn't he? Inspector! Didn't he?"

Kipper couldn't get away fast enough. He couldn't help thinking that Bigby and his bunch of bastards would have handled the interview differently.

Seventeen

I don't know, they say there's no rest for the wicked or the beautiful – some guff of that nature anyway. The point I'm making is that there I was, stretched out on me bunk, thinking I may as well make myself comfortable, when a copper comes along and disturbs my shuteye by turning a key in the lock and shoving the door open with an almighty clang. Well, I damn near jumped out of my skin and it amused the copper and he tells me to stop messing about on account of there was somebody wanting to see me.

"Hoo?" I asked, sitting up.

"I don't know who she is," the copper shrugged. "Your Mrs, she says."

"My—" I shut my trap. It wasn't Doctor Hoo, then. It was some bint claiming to be my old lady. Well, it was some sort of mistake on account of I ain't never been married. I've been to prison once so there's no way I'm signing up for another one.

Well, this copper had piqued my interest, hadn't he? So I got to my plates and set my clothes straight and ran a hand over my hair.

"How do I look?" I arsked him but he just sneered and said, "With your bleedin' eyes, mate," and he led me away, back to that room – or one very much like it, where there was a table and a couple of chairs. On one of them chairs sat the bint in question, all starched blouse and hooks and eyes rather than buttons. She had on her loaf a titfer, a black straw boater what had a red carnation on it. It was the only bit of colour on her. She stared at me when I came in, steely-eyed and grim. I had never seen her before in my life.

"Hello, love," I winked and pulled out my chair.

"What is this?" she squawked like a parrot stuck under a door. She got to her feet. She addressed her question to the copper who was standing guard in case she tried to pass me a cake with a file in it or something.

"Is there a problem?" said the copper.

"Sit down, darlin'," I told her. "Take the weight off."

She pointed at me but kept her eyes on the copper. "Who is this?" she demanded. Well, 'who' was a step up from 'what', I supposed.

"It's your husband," said the copper.

"It bloody well isn't," said the woman, glancing at me with a sneer of disdain. "You've brung me the wrong one."

"No, I haven't," said the copper. "This is him all right. This is Jedidiah Plank."

The scandalised look on the woman's face was enough to make me feel insulted.

"Look at him," she said. "Do you think I'd wed my soul to a pasty-faced whippersnapper like that?"

"Hoi!" I said on account of there being nobody else to stick up for me. "You're no oil painting yourself."

"Now, now," said the copper. "Don't go having a domestic."

At that the woman roared. I reckon she was seconds away from swinging for that copper.

"Young man," she said, struggling to retain her temper. "You are quite mistaken. This – stripling – is not my husband. This is not Jedidiah Plank."

"No?" said the copper.

"After twenty years you get to know what someone looks like. And this boy doesn't even look twenty!"

"Oh. Well, if you're sure… Only the fingerprints…"

I almost felt sorry for that copper and would have, were it not for the fact that he was a copper. He didn't know what to make of it all. He stood gawping like a stunned goldfish for a bit, his face getting redder and redder by the second, and then he comes to a decision and he says, "Right. Sit down, both of you. I'll go and fetch the sergeant." And before we could say boo, off he goes but he ain't completely stupid: he locked the bleedin' door behind him. He shouldn't have done that, leaving a criminal and a member of the public alone together so I reckoned he was in for a dressing-down from his sergeant, but of the two of us, me and the bint, I reckoned I was in the most danger. I felt like old Brutus in the lions' cage.

The woman – Mrs Plank, I suppose she was – sat down again, keeping the table between us. She bored into me with her eyes and I felt a twinge of sympathy or something for the original owner of my chalks, having to come home to that.

"Who are you?" she said. "Why do these idiots seem to think you are my husband?"

I nodded at the empty chair. She nodded too, allowing me to sit on it.

"Listen, Mrs," I began, although she wasn't making it no easier for me, "About your husband. I think he's brown bread."

"What are you talking about?"

"He's popped his clogs, Mrs. Folded his umbrella." I was trying to break it to the poor cow as sensitively as I could. "He's snuffed it."

"Clogs? Snuffed? Umbrella? You're a blithering idiot." And then it dawned on her. "Are you telling me my husband is dead?"

"It looks that way, yes."

"And – and – where is he? What happened? Is he here?" The steely look in her eyes had been replaced by panic and pain and I began to feel sorry for her.

"Not exactly," I said. "Listen, how did you know to come here?"

She frowned as though she didn't understand the question and her eyes brimmed with tears and I thought, Oh gawd.

"Do you know," she said, her lips quivering. "It was the queerest thing. I got a message."

"Who from?"

"That's just it; I don't know. A note was pushed under the door. I opened it – the door, I mean but there was nobody there. But I did catch a glimpse of somebody over the road. Somebody tall and rather gaunt. Chinese he might have been. And then an omnibus came by and when it had moved on again, he was gone."

Doctor Hoo!

"And what did it say, this note?"

"It didn't say much. Just 'husband' and 'Bow Street'."

He always was a man of few words.

"So I came along, thinking what's he got himself into this time. Oh, I try to keep him on the straight and narrow but it's not easy. Where is he? Oh, that's right. You said he was dead."

Poor cow.

She reached across the table and took my hand in both of hers and gave it a right old squeeze. Tears were spilling down her face and her eyes searched for mine through their watery curtain. "Were you with him at the end?"

"Er—"

And then her expression changed. She looked at my hand and turned it over. Puzzled bewilderment clouded her boat, like she recognised something and she didn't like it. She shoved my hand away and got to her feet, knocking her chair over.

She proceeded to scream the place down.

I did my best to shush her but she kept screaming and backing away, and the copper came in, bringing the bushy-bearded sergeant with him and they grabbed me by the arms. So rough they was I thought they was going to have my chalks right off – as if I was the one causing the commotion.

"That's not my husband!" the woman kept screaming.

They bundled me out of there sharpish and bunged me back in the cell.

"You can wait in here until we find out what to do with you," said Bushy-Beard.

115

The other copper rolled his eyes at me and he says, well, he says, if you ain't Damien Deacus and you ain't Jedidiah Plank, who the bleedin' hell are you?

And he goes, giving the door a slam.

Actually, I could have said, I'm a bit of both.

Eighteen

Kipper found Bow Street nick overrun with men from Scotland Yard. *Like an infestation of vermin,* he sneered. *Vermin that won't stop talking to me.*

That rat, Bigby, clapped his arm around Kipper's shoulder in greeting. It was becoming a habit almost as nauseating as his perpetual pipe-smoking.

"Johnny!" Bigby cried as if reunited with a long-lost friend. "Hope you don't mind us moving in like this."

"Moving in?" Kipper's jaw dropped like a broken drawbridge.

"Making here the base of our operations."

"Scotland Yard burn down, did it?" A note of hope ignited Kipper's eyes.

"Here is more convenient," said Bigby. "We don't mind roughing it. And, if all goes to plan, we shall be out of your hair before you can say Jack Robinson."

"Who?"

"Idiomatic expression. Don't worry about it."

"'Plan'?"

"We haven't just stopped by for tea and crumpets, old boy – speaking of which…"

A cheer went up as Sergeant Adams elbowed his way in, bearing a tea tray that rattled with cups and saucers.

"Good man, your sergeant," Bigby nudged Kipper. "I've half a mind to poach him."

You can boil him in oil for all I care, Kipper glowered in Adams's direction. *The traitor!*

Bigby accepted a cup of tea with a gracious nod. "What's this? No crumpets?"

"Only muffins, I'm afraid, sir," Sergeant Adams looked bashful. "I could send Constable Harding—"

"No, no need," Bigby took up a buttered muffin and bit into it with gusto. "Lovely."

"Sir?" Adams offered the tray to Kipper.

"Good god, no. This is a place of work not the bleedin' Savoy."

Downcast, Adams shuffled away.

"Right," said Kipper. "You had better tell me what you and your tea-swilling, muffin munchers are doing in my nick."

Bigby smirked, amused. "Muffin munchers! I like that. Makes us sound like a load of lesbians."

"Who?" said Kipper. "No!" he stamped his foot. "Tell me what you're doing or bugger off out of it."

Bigby laughed and rested a buttock on the edge of a desk. "Pooling resources, old boy. Putting our heads together. Many hands make light work and all of that, what!"

Kipper frowned, none the wiser.

"Two heads, better than one? No? Never heard that one either? Honestly, Johnny: we could use your acuity on this one."

"Me what?"

"Your finely-tuned copper's instinct. This place is handy for our sting, to be sure, but it also has the additional benefit of having you here, Inspector John Kipper. Your name carries a lot of weight."

"Does it?"

"Oh, yes! I'll say!"

Kipper stood up straight. Well, I never! He coughed, embarrassed. "Hang about!" he cleared his throat. "You said something about a sting?"

Bigby marvelled. "There it is! Mind like a steel trap. We're going undercover, Johnny, setting a snare for old Foggy Jack, lure him out into the open and then—" He clapped his hands right in front of Kipper's nose, "We've got the fiend!"

Kipper, blushing to have been so startled, backed off a little. "Fiend? That's a bit…"

"Is it? I was going to go with 'bastard' but no, I think 'fiend' is better. Now, let me tell you what we have in mind."

Nineteen

It looked like I was going to be there for the night. Doctor Hoo's plan, as far as I could tell was to get me sprung from the nick by having Plank's Mrs tell the coppers they'd got the wrong man. Well, it wasn't going too well so far, was it?

I stretched out on the bunk again, wrapping the rough blanket around me and tried not to feel sorry for myself.

I can tell you that cell didn't get no more comfortable or inviting the longer I spent in it but, somehow, despite my thoughts racing each other to the front of my mind, I found myself drifting off to sleep. You know how it is when your thinking blends in with your dreams until you don't know what's what no more.

Well, I was thinking about Doctor Hoo and how his plan to get me out of there by having Plank's Mrs tell 'em I wasn't who they thought I was, and what he'd try next to get me out of there, and I was kicking myself for being a bloody fool for not trusting the doctor in the first place and how could I thought for one second that he was turning me in to the rozzers. And I remembered trying to climb out of the window with me new chalks letting me down and then – them eyes! That pair of minces looking in at me and laughing and—

Blow me, if they weren't there again!

There in the dark, in my cell, what had, I remind you, a bleedin' locked door!

I sat up on my bunk and rubbed my eyes but they was still there, staring at me. I held the blanket, clinging to it like it would shield me from this horror. My skin was crawling, tingling with a childlike terror I hadn't felt since I was a nipper.

It was a dream. It had to be.

"Piss off," I told my visitor. It didn't piss off. It laughed. It stayed where it bleedin' was and laughed. I got more annoyed with it than scared, to be honest.

"Who are you?" It seemed reasonable to arsk. "And how did you get in here?"

The shadows moved and, as well as the eyes, I could make out the size and the shape of my uninvited guest. It couldn't have been no more than a yard or so in height. A child, then. Or a midget. Either way: too big to get in through the bleedin' keyhole.

"Hello, Damien," says the midget-child in a high voice but I can't tell if it's Benny or Jenny.

"Here!" I objected. "How'd you know my name?"

"It's written on the door," laughed the little titch. "But I've been watching you for a long time."

"Oh, yes?" I was glad of the darkness; it hid my blushes. "Even earlier on when I availed myself of the bucket?"

"Long before then," said the tiddler. "You're quite a character."

"Oh, am I indeed? Well, if you're going to come in here, calling me that, and spying on me private moments, don't you think you ought to introduce yourself?"

"I am doing," said the short-arse. "Call me Sprite."

"Funny name."

"Sorry to disappoint."

"Oh, no, I'm not disappointed. I mean it's not like I thought you was, for example, the Ghost with the Christmas Present or nothing like that. Now, are you going to piss off like I told you or tell me what the bleedin' hell you want?"

I felt I could speak so boldly to this Sprite figure an account of it being nothing but a dream, brung about by me having had no supper. I ought to complain about that, I had.

"Both," said Sprite, "but not in that order. Your employer."

"Who?"

"Exactly. He is a remarkable man."

"That's one way to describe him."

"I have need of his services."

"What? D'you need a new pair of chalks and all? Perhaps he's still got me old ones knocking around."

"No, no. Not those services."

"What then?"

"Not now, not yet."

"When then?"

"Ssh!" He or she (I don't bleedin' know) pressed a dirty finger to my lips. It didn't half pong and I dreaded to think where it might have been. "You don't need to know."

I shrank back and wiped the back of my hand across my cakehole and then spat on the floor for good measure. "Then why come here? Why tell me anything at all?"

But the Sprite thing was gone. Just vanished. I looked under my blanket and even in the bucket to make sure.

There was fat chance of sleep after that. I lay awake until the morning, trying to work out if I'd woken up before the visit or after.

Twenty

Kipper waited in the fog. He wondered if the 'fiend' was waiting too. Perhaps he was close, perhaps waiting and watching too. The lights of the public house on the corner glowed a dim yellow and the murk muffled the sounds of the last straggling drinkers. The heels of a woman's shoes clicked and clattered on the cobblestones. The wearer was negotiating prices with her client: a tanner in the hand or a bob in the mouth. The client was silent; Kipper supposed it must be a gentleman who did not wish to be overheard discussing such ungentlemanly things in the squalid Whitechapel streets.

Kipper found himself holding his breath until the pair had passed by to conduct their transaction in some other alley. Perhaps it would be over quickly and the dollymop would come back this way on her Molly, hoping to pick up one last punter as the pub closed its doors.

Out of the gloom came another figure, along with the odour of cheap lavender water. Kipper pressed his back against the wall, heedless of the damp seeping through his coat. The last thing he wanted was to draw attention to himself by having to fend off a grubby business proposition. His heart pounded like galloping hooves against his ribs. He continued to hold his breath and his fingers tightened their grip on the police-issue revolver in his pocket. He hadn't wanted it, had never fired one, but Bigby had insisted. Even the sight of it, he'd told Kipper, might give our fiend pause and that might be enough for us to nab him. Kipper didn't share Bigby's confidence that things would be as cut and dried as all that but it was comforting, he would admit, to have the firearm in his possession. Just in case.

The perfumed figure was a tall woman in a tattered red shawl. Her hair was piled high above a pale and painted face. She tripped and tottered from a little too much gin. If I was Foggy Jack, Kipper mused, she'd be just the kind of mark I'd be looking for... He shuddered, revolted. He didn't want to think like a killer – like a fiend! – but Bigby suggested it would be useful to see things through Foggy Jack's eyes.

Kipper watched the woman go by. Finer details were visible to him now: the paste earrings, the beauty spot on her cheek, the blue five o'clock shadow—

What the hell?

The shape of a man stepped out of the fog, stopping the woman in her tracks. Kipper saw a glint of steel as the man, barely more than a silhouette, brandished a cutthroat razor.

"Put your hands up, dearie!" scoffed a voice Kipper recognised as that of the first dollymop. The man wheeled around to find the whore and her gentleman client pointing pistols at his chest. The whore in the red shawl drew out a truncheon. She peeled off her wig and scratched at her undeniably male haircut.

"Gaw', that don't half itch."

"Never mind that, Sergeant," said the gentleman in the unmistakable tones of Bigby of the Yard. "Cuff the bastard and let's get him down Bow Street nick."

The fiend let out a roar of outrage. He swirled his cloak and slashed at the air with his razor, keeping the undercover coppers at bay. "Fools!" he snarled and his eyes flashed red beneath the brim of his top hat. "Your prisons cannot hold me."

"They won't have to, old love," said Bigby. "You'll be having your neck stretched before you can blink."

The fiend threw back his head and laughed. His arm darted out and he cut the first whore's throat. She fired her gun as she fell – the shot went wide and glanced off a lamppost. Bigby's gun would not fire. A tendril of fog curled around the nozzle, yanked the weapon from his hand and hurled it down the street. The fiend slashed at Bigby, opening a gash in his cheek. Sergeant Adams – for it was he in the red shawl – stood his ground although Kipper could see his truncheon wobbling. Drawing his gun, Kipper strode forth to defend his sergeant.

Foggy Jack saw him coming and laughed again. Then he took everyone by surprise by dissolving into the fog – the laughter was the last to go – leaving the police one man down, empty-handed and more than a little stupefied.

"What happened?" gasped Kipper. "Where did he go?"

"Melted into air," said Sergeant Adams with a faraway expression, "Into thin air."

Kipper gaped at the man, not least because he had never seen Adams clean-shaven before, let alone in female attire.

Bigby knelt by the body of his fallen colleague (a Scotland Yard bloke by the name of Darby). Kipper offered him a folded handkerchief to staunch the gaping wound on his face. They stared at the spot where the fiend had been, within reach, within their grasp.

If one can grasp fog, that is.

The fiend had got clean away. Foggy Jack was free to strike again.

***

It took several stitches to fix Bigby's cheek. The barber-surgeon advised him it would scar.

"Rather!" Bigby liked the idea. "A memento of my encounter with Foggy Jack. A close shave, you might say, what!"

Kipper's mood was less ebullient. "I don't know how you can be so chipper," he complained. "He got away. I say 'he' but I mean 'it'. That weren't no human we saw tonight."

Bigby stared at him and sucked contemplatively on his pipe. "Good lord, man, I do believe you're serious."

"I am!" said Kipper. "Foggy Jack ain't a man."

"Oh? Then what is he?"

"You said it yourself: he's a fiend."

Bigby chuckled as though a child had said something inadvertently amusing. "It's just a word, old boy. Like one might say 'opium fiend' or 'gambling fiend.'"

"Pipe-smoking fiend?"

"Ha, ha! Yes, exactly. Figurative language, old bean. Not to be taken literally."

"Yes, but," said Kipper, "if he ain't no actual fiend, what is he? Where did he appear from? Where did he disappear to? And how did he get away? You saw it, same as I did. Same as Sergeant Adams did. How did he vanish like that?"

Bigby sighed, like a long-suffering parent having to explain something to a dim-witted offspring. "Well, clearly," he puffed at his pipe, "It's magic. Now, don't get too excited and let the idea run away with you, Johnny. When I say 'magic' I mean 'conjuring tricks' of the sort one may see at any old music hall any night of the week. Think about it, man. Top hat and cloak. No stage magician worth his salt would be without them."

Kipper's jaw dropped. Bigby's idea had merit and gained in plausibility the more he thought about it.

"Misdirection, old boy," Bigby patted Kipper's upper arm. "Oldest trick in the book of old tricks. Now, I must be off to Cricklewood to break the sad news to Darby's widow – although I'll neglect to mention the part about him being dressed up as a tart, what! Then I'd best show my face at home, let the wife know I haven't left her. I say, do you have a little woman waiting for you, Johnny?"

"No," Kipper muttered. "No woman of any size."

"Well, you should get one," Bigby advised. "Can get terribly lonely, can police work. Ta-ta!"

He left Kipper's office with a jaunty salute. Kipper sat down heavily and thumped his blotter. The nerve of the man. And how the hell did a back-to-front like Bigby manage to bamboozle some poor cow into marrying him? It beggared belief.

"Tea, sir!" Sergeant Adams breezed in with a tray. "It's perked me up no end."

Kipper stared at the sergeant's denuded face. "You look about nine years old," he observed.

"Thank you, sir."

"And for gawd's sake, get back into uniform. That frock is doing nobody any favours."

Sergeant Adams blushed. His face and neck turned red so it was almost as though his beard was back. Kipper felt terrible; Adams had been through an ordeal, had bravely faced the fiend at close quarters.

"Sergeant, I'll need a list—"

"Done already, sir. List of all the conjurors currently working in London theatres and music halls, sir."

Kipper marvelled. "How did—"

"Stands to reason, don't it, sir? Our man's a magician, ain't he? Disappearing like that. Think about it, sir. They uses blades and all. Sawing women in half. Plunging swords through wicker baskets. Chucking knives at bints on spinning wheels."

"Good god," Kipper blinked. "That ain't total nonsense."

Adams grinned, brimming with pride. "Thank you, sir."

"And that berk Bigby didn't put you up to this?"

"Oh, no, sir! I just used me loaf, sir. Stands to reason."

"Sit down, Sergeant. Join me in a cuppa. I'll be mother."

While Kipper poured, Sergeant Adams lowered himself onto a chair, taking care not to crease his dollymop's frock.

"You're a good man, Adams," Kipper offered the sugar bowl, "Despite appearances to the contrary."

Twenty-One

Of course, being shut up in a cell on your Jack Jones gives you a lot of time to think. Well, there ain't much else to do apart from counting the bricks in the wall. I was itching to get out – of course I was – but the longer I stayed there, the lower my spirits sank and I got to thinking perhaps I deserved to be there after all, on account of I had killed a man. Well, my brief had put it differently in court. He said a man was dead because of me, which ain't quite the same thing, apart from the end result. But the jury was having none of it. They came back with a guilty verdict. I was guilty of murder, said the judge. Manslaughter was out of the question and no sop to the dead man's widow and nippers, therefore I was to be hanged by the neck until I was brown bread and there was an end to it – an end to yours truly.

Only, of course, it wasn't, or you wouldn't be reading of my further adventures now, would you?

I remember the day in question vividly, although I tries not to dwell on it. It's like a painting in your house or a favourite story from when you was a kiddie. You can recall every detail as well as your own name and it's always there in your head. You can walk past that picture every day and not look at it but you know it's there. And being banged up like I was, I had plenty of time to stop and look at that picture all over again.

It happened in the market down Portobello Road. Doctor Hoo had sent me out to pick up a few bits. I think he just wanted me out from under his feet, truth be told. He'd been working on something-or-other up in his lab, only I weren't privy to it, but then he's always been a secretive bugger at the best of times. It turned out to be them brass fittings what's on that toff's leg and, let us not forget, is holding me new chalks to me old shoulders; I only found this out after I was dug up. Anyway, off I went to the market with a list of bits and bobs to get. Broken clocks mainly, it looked like, and who was I to question it?

Only I hadn't even made it to the first bleedin' stall when some ruffian grabs me by the arm – one of me old ones – and shoves me into an alley and into a pile of boxes – you know the kind greengrocers have, the sort they carries their apples and pears in – and this time I really do mean apples and pears, not their bleedin' stairs because that wouldn't make no sense, would it? There was a stack of them piled up and he throws me into them and they breaks under me. Well, they're only thin wood, ain't they, and light? While I'm trying to pull myself up and keep out of his reach, he pulls a knife and kicks me legs from under me so I lands on me Aris' again and I'm sure a splinter of that wood goes right up me jacksy.

The ruffian's after the dosh, of course, and he holds his hand out for it but I tells him what he can go and do to himself as an alternative, which only serves to enrage him and he starts swinging his arm about – the one that's holding the knife, of course – and I scrambles away, backwards, like I'm a bleedin' crab trying to escape from Billingsgate but I'm only getting farther and farther into the alley, trapping myself good and proper.

"Give me your money!" he barks, jabbing in my direction with his knife and he's bearing down on me and blocking out the light in that alley and all I can think of is Doctor bleedin' Hoo and what he'll do if I goes back empty-handed, and that's a million times more scary than what this knife-wielding prick might do to me and I thinks, No! I ain't going to let it happen, so I charges at the robber, like a bull at a – well, like a bull charging at anything, really – and it takes him completely by surprise to have my head butting into his belly, and I'm roaring like one of them old circus lions when they found Brutus in their midst, and I drives the robber backwards, toward the mouth of the alley, and it all happens so bleedin' fast. Over he falls, down he goes, right on his back, and he lands on them wooden boxes, just like I had, only they wasn't already broken when I had my go, and there's a big, sharp shard, only I don't see it and neither does he, not until it's sticking out of the front of his shirt. We both looks at it in surprise and our eyes are wide and his locks on mine and it occurs to me to apologise and it occurs to him to spill blood from out his mouth and he lies back and dies and he drops his knife and me, not thinking straight, I picks up the knife and I offers it to him, thinking that might make things right. And then a woman screams and the mouth of the alley is blocked by a crowd and a whistle blows and the coppers turn up to take me away…

As far as the coppers was concerned, it was an open-and-shut case. There was plenty of witnesses who opened their gobs in a rush to tell the police what they thought they had seen, and then it was a matter of the coppers shutting the cell door.

Nobody had seen the robber accost me. I should be so bleedin' lucky. All anybody saw was me standing over him with a knife in my hand and blood coming out of his belly. Then they found I had money in my pocket and they thought that *I* had robbed *him*! I tried to show them me shopping list as the reason why I had so much cash but I couldn't find it. I must have bleedin' dropped it in the alley. Well, I couldn't tell him to speak to my employer on account of Doctor Hoo liking his business kept quiet and all that. So I didn't have a peg to stand on, did I?

So I was done for murder and robbery with violence and my fate was sealed. Well, I've told you how Doctor Hoo got me out of that – eventually! – because that's where you came in; but now that I was back behind bars, I was preparing myself for a long stretch – and I don't mean my neck because I don't think they was going to hang me again but I had a feeling they didn't know what to do with me, so I was going to be left to rot in prison. Well, it's what I would have done if I was in their ones and twos.

And then, just as I'm getting settled in, under that scratchy blanket and feeling sorrier for myself than a pirate with woodworm, the cell door opened and a man in a frock tells me I am free to go.

Twenty-Two

"Somebody to see you, sir."

Kipper looked up from his notes and glared. Sergeant Adams was still wearing his dollymop costume. Adams caught the glare and apologised.

"I was just about to get changed, sir – I've had to send a cab to Scotland Yard to pick up me uniform, but I thought you'd want to see him right away, sir."

"Who?"

"That's right, sir! How did you guess?"

Kipper scowled. Adams actually bobbed in a curtsey and scurried out. Kipper got to his feet as a tall, slender figure appeared in the doorway. He gasped involuntarily as the lamplight played on the visitor's features.

It's a mask! It has to be! The thought arose again like desperate hope. Nobody could really look like that. Could they?

"Come in." Kipper managed to squeak. He cleared his throat and made a gesture of invitation. The man stepped over the threshold without seeming to move at all. He seemed taller in the office; Kipper waved vaguely at a chair but the man declined the offer – but how exactly he did this, Kipper could not say. Kipper felt uncomfortable in his chair with the visitor towering over him so he stood up again. It helped but not much.

"What can I do for you, Hoo?"

It might have been the inspector's imagination but he could have sworn Hoo's lips curled in a lop-sided smile. Not a mask, then; the poor bleeder really does look like that.

"Deacus," Hoo's voice rumbled from somewhere deep inside him.

"I beg yours," said Kipper. "Oh, oh! Him! What about him?"

"Release him."

Kipper emitted a laugh of surprise. "I should cocoa. Go on, get out of it. Coming in here. He's a convicted murderer, that one."

Hoo's lips parted enough to give Kipper a flash of his small but even teeth.

"Verdict unsound," he said. "Accident."

"Now, look here," Kipper, more than a little unnerved, wanted rid of this eerie presence and sharpish. "Bit late to come in here, defending him. Doctor of Law, are you? Where was you when the trial was going on then, eh? Go on; sling your hook."

But Doctor Hoo showed no signs of going anywhere. In fact, to Kipper he looked like he had planted himself in the office like a lamppost or a tree – No – a totem pole.

"Foggy Jack," said Hoo and Kipper's blood ran cold.

"What about him?"

"Release Deacus. I catch killer."

Kipper gasped in disbelief. "Oh, no! Oh, no! It don't work like that. What? Make me a deal, will you? I don't know you from Adam."

Hoo stared, implacable. He touched his hat and left. Sergeant Adams materialised in the doorway.

"Excuse me, sir, Doctor, only there's a message come from Bigby of the Yard, sir. Wants to know if you wants to join him talking to a coachload of them stage magicians."

Kipper groaned. Bigby was ahead of the game again, was he? Got a head start with the conjurors and I'm expected to tag along, am I?

Sod that for a game of soldiers.

Kipper looked from Adams to the space vacated by Hoo and back again. "Tell him thanks but no thanks."

"Right you are, sir."

"And Adams?"

"Yes, sir? Uniform's on its way, sir."

"Never mind that. Pop down to the cells, will you, and give our friend Deacus his liberty."

***

"There's no need for this, Inspector. I can find me own way home and I won't dilly-dally on the way, neither."

Damien Deacus fidgeted in his seat in the cab the copper in the frock had summoned.

"I'm sure you can find your way to a lot of places," Kipper's smile was taut and humourless. "To Limehouse, please, driver!"

"Ta-ta, sir," Sergeant Adams simpered from the footpath. Kipper reddened.

"Get back inside, man!" he urged. "Before somebody clocks you."

Deacus sniggered. "It's him, ain't it? The one what had the beard."

Kipper glowered at him and was almost jolted from his seat as the cab moved off.

"And I thought I kept strange company," Deacus laughed. Kipper scowled, sparing himself the futility of trying to explain about Adams's undercover garb. A toe rag like Deacus would not appreciate the finer points of police work.

Their journey continued in silence, save for the horses' hooves on the cobbles and the sounds of the streets, which became quieter the closer they drew to the docks. The hour was late and it seemed even the smugglers were having an hour or two off.

"He's a right one, isn't he?" Kipper prompted.

Deacus frowned. "Who is?"

"Your boss."

"Is he? That's one word for it."

"It's two words, actually."

"I suppose he is."

134

"What?"

"A right one. His heart's in the right place."

"Is it?"

"Yeah. It's on the inside. Really, Inspector, I'm touched you would bring me all the way out here and I'm thankful for the escort – don't think I'm not – but I can walk it from here; it ain't far."

Deacus made to get up but a bark from the inspector sat him down again. "Stay where you are!" Kipper snapped. "Before we go in, you're going to tell me everything you know about this Doctor Hoo."

"Am I?"

"Or we could turn this cab around and deliver you back to the nick."

"Oh."

"Yes," said Kipper. "Oh."

Twenty-Three

Well, I should have bleedin' known. I should have known my liberty would come with strings attached. I had to think carefully and quick. What could I tell this copper that wouldn't land me nor Hoo in the tom tit?

"He's a doctor, ain't he?" I shrugged. "Didn't he give you one of his cards?"

The copper let out a grunt what I think was meant to signify 'yes'.

"But he no longer practises?"

"Oh, he's practising all the bleedin' time, mate. That's why he's so good at it."

The copper – Inspector Fishface, I'll call him – was not amused.

"But his Harley Street premises are shut up."

"He's moved out. No law against it, is there?"

"My question is why."

"Well, you'll have to arsk him about that, won't you?"

"I will."

"Good luck to you."

"Been with him long?"

"How'd you mean?"

"In his employ."

"Years, mate. Man and boy."

"Tell me about it."

I sat back. Old Fishface had got the cab driving around in circles, delaying our arrival at the warehouse. Clever bastard. He could have arsked me all this back at the nick and I wouldn't have said nothing. But out here, on the streets where I could taste the air of freedom, he was showing me what I was in danger of losing all over again. Like I said: clever bastard.

***

Doctor Hoo was hard at it when I brung Fishface up to the lab. "Just don't touch nothing," I warned him. "He don't like it if you touches his things."

Old Fishface muttered something about being of a similar disposition and I couldn't tell if he was trying to be funny.

True to form, the doctor's workbench was littered with clock parts. Dials, cogs, and wheels was all over the shop, and the doctor was wearing his goggles with the magnifying lenses what made his minces looks like somebody peeping through a letterbox. He was concentrating hard on something fiddly so I put my hand out to keep the inspector at bay until a suitable interval arose. When Hoo had finished what he was doing, I didn't have to clear my throat nor nothing. He knew we was there and he said, Good evening, before he turned around – When he turned it was peculiar; he just sort of revolved like a little figure in a music box I once nicked – I mean, saw in a window. (I've got to be careful what I think with Fishface at my elbow, in case anything incriminating slips out me north). I see the effect Hoo's strangeness has on the copper.

"You'll get used to it," I says out the side of my mouth. Which was a bit of a falsehood on account of I ain't never got used to it.

"Come," says Hoo and he picks up the lantern and we has to follow him pretty sharpish or get left in the dark.

He stopped at a covered object in a far corner, and waited for us to catch up.

"What is this?" said Fishface with impatience. He'd come to talk about catching a killer not to witness some kind of bleedin' unveiling ceremony.

"See," said Doctor Hoo and he lifted up a corner of the tarpaulin and slowly pulled it away, revealing a tall crate, almost a coffin, really – especially when you saw there was somebody standing up in it. A woman. Tarted up like a two-penny dollymop.

"My Gawd," said Fishface, peering closer. I did too. "I don't understand."

Neither did I, to tell you the truth, only I didn't say nothing, on account of not wanting the copper to know I was in the dark as much as he was.

"Bait," said Doctor Hoo.

"Come again?" said Fishface.

"Bait," said Doctor Hoo a second time.

"Stands to reason," I chipped in. "It's bait, ain't it?"

Kipper took a break from staring at the dollymop long enough to send me a puzzled look, and then he went back to gawping at the woman in the box again.

She was an amazing piece of work and no mistake. Lifelike, except she wasn't breathing. The detail was astonishing. From the make-up caked on her cheeks to the bruises on her shins, Hoo had not overlooked a thing.

I saw him, watching us, and even he couldn't hide the smile of pride on his mush. If I had a minute alone with him I would have arsked him what he was playing at, but I had to keep shtum on account of the copper being right there.

Speaking of him: Fishface's fingers was reaching slowly toward the dollymop's arm.

"No touch!" said Hoo.

"What did I tell you?" I said, but Fishface took no bleedin' notice. His fingertips touched the dollymop's arm, gingerly at first, as though he was afraid she would wake up, and then he got a little bolder and he's trying to pinch and squeeze her. Then he's rapping on the arm with his knuckles and it makes a hollow sound, so he tries again on her chest and it makes a deeper sound.

Well, I pulls him away before he launches into a drum solo. At least I've got one question answered: she weren't made out of no dead bodies, which had been my first thought.

"I don't get it," said Kipper, pushing me away from him. "What's all this in aid of?"

"Bait," said Hoo, and I could tell that even his patience was wearing thin.

And then it clicked.

"Don't you get it?" I teased the copper. "This here dollymop's a decoy. We put her out on the street and along comes Foggy Jack and we nab him. Or rather, you do, on account of it being your bleedin' job and all."

Fishface looked far from convinced. He stroked his chin and squinted at the dollymop. "I don't know," he said. "Even with a ton of fog…"

Something else clicked – and not in my loaf this time. Something whirred as well, and the dollymop's eyes flew open and she was looking right at him with bright baby blues. Her mouth opened but didn't move as words came out of it. "Tanner in the hand and a bob in the gob," she said.

Fishface recoiled but he was clearly fascinated. "Good Gawd!" he said.

"I know," I chuckled. "Prices ain't half gone up."

***

We called it Coppélia after the puppet in the old story and we passed a couple of amusing hours in her company, seeing what she could do.

She could walk, after a fashion; she staggered like a drunkard wearing leg splints, lurching and listing alarmingly. We decided pretty sharpish we couldn't let her out to walk the streets like that. Instead, we would station her somewhere, propped up against a lamppost or something in a come-hither pose, 'cause she weren't half alluring. In a certain light. There was something about the way her eyelids half-closed and her lips barely parted – I could see the inspector was quite taken with her, while I was just appreciating Hoo's craftsmanship – of course I was.

She could move her hands, by which I mean they could rotate at the wrist but her fingers didn't work independently. It was all or nothing where her fingers was concerned; she could clasp money in her palms but then she didn't know what to do with it.

Her speech was limited to a few phrases that Hoo had recorded in some way – don't arsk me how, but I reckon it was something like them rolls of paper you pop in a pianola, with holes in that play the tune as it goes through the machinery. Or the cylinder in a music box, with raised bumps on it. Come to think of it, our Coppélia was a bit like them little ballerinas you sometimes get in a music box, standing on one leg in front of tiny mirrors – and come to think of something else, I think there's even a ballet with the same name as our tin trollop.

Because that's what she was made of, not sugar and spice, and definitely not the stitched together bits and bobs of dug-up bodies. Doctor Hoo had really surpassed himself with this one. He'd stretched thin rubber over her and painted it so it looked like skin. And of course the hair was a wig and the eyelashes was real false eyelashes, and her face was painted up just like any other whore's, so on the whole, there weren't that much extra about Coppélia that was falser than any other dollymop, if you want to look at it like that.

As far as speaking was concerned, the copper said she shouldn't utter a word if somebody was looking right at her, on account of her lips not moving, only her jaw going up and down like a ventriloquist's dummy's. She needed to move just enough and speak just enough to give the impression that she was a living human person, waiting outside an alley, and not a statue in honour of prostitutes.

He weren't half excited, that copper. His eyes was bright with the possibilities of what Coppélia could do.

"We ain't putting nobody at risk," he said. "None of my men has to dress up and no real dollymop is in danger."

Doctor Hoo, he stood back, watching us with his dollymop dolly. He didn't make no notes nor nothing but I could tell he was taking it all in and – what was that? – Could it be a hint of pride on his usually blank face? Well, my hat was off to him.

"This will revolutionise police work," old Fishface paced up and down but his plates couldn't catch up with his loaf. His thoughts was running away with him.

And then he stopped, all of a sudden, as though something had struck him. Or he's struck something, like walking into a pane of glass.

"How does it work, your miraculous invention? Is it a puppet? Do you have to be near her? Is that it?"

He searched Hoo's face but of course it was like trying to read a blank sheet of paper. The doctor put his hand into his lab coat pocket and he took out a key, very like the one I told you about before, with a butterfly head. Kipper the copper plucked it from Hoo's gloved fingers and examined it.

"Clockwork! Of course!"

Yeah, bleedin'obvious when you think about it.

Hoo turned Coppélia around – in a rather ungentlemanly fashion, if you arsks me – and unlaced her bodice. Rows of keyholes was revealed, up and down her back. Hoo pointed at them in turn.

"Eyes," he said. "Hands. Mouth. Left arm. Right arm. So on."

Fishface tried the key in a couple of the holes. It fitted them all. Coppélia straightened and her gob began to flap. Her eyes rolled in opposite directions and her hands chopped the air. Hoo's hand stayed Kipper's.

"Too tight," he rumbled. Kipper looked embarrassed, like a kiddie told off for breaking his new toy on Christmas morning – Well, I'm imagining this, on account of I ain't never had no toys on Christmas morning nor any other morning neither. But put away your violin and save any tears you might have for me for later.

The copper swears – he even crosses his heart but I don't think that makes a blind bit of difference to Doctor Hoo – he swears and promises that he'll be careful and treat Coppélia with the respect she deserves. He couldn't wait to get started. I don't know why he was in so much of a rush but somehow I don't reckon it was concern for another dollymop – a real live flesh and blood one – that was spurring him on.

I looked at Inspector Kipper with fresh eyes. Turns out you're a bit of strange one too, ain't you?

Twenty-Four

Inspector Kipper thought they had better wait a few nights before putting Coppélia to use. The killer would no doubt be wary after the police's last botched attempt. Kipper could only hope no more dollymops would fall foul of Foggy Jack in the interim. Every morning, Kipper dreaded news of another victim but, mercifully, there was none. Bigby accredited the lack of new murders to having the killer in custody; he had rounded up every stage magician in London and was in the process of whittling them down. Kipper went along to observe a couple of Bigby's interrogations, which were little more than private demonstrations of the magicians' art.

"Tight-lipped bunch, these prestidigitators, what!" Bigby pressed new teeth marks into the stem of his pipe. "Not giving anything away. One might suspect a conspiracy."

"Shouldn't think so," Kipper shrugged. "They're all under oath, I shouldn't wonder, not to reveal how their tricks are done. They daren't breathe a word or else they'll be for the chop. Or the saw. Or the sword through the loaf."

Bigby blinked. "You amaze me. So, I've got a right bunch of c – conjurors, shall we say? All keeping mum because of some professional code of conduct."

"That's about the size of it," Kipper tried not to laugh. "You'd have been better off going to see them in their natural habitat."

"What do you mean?"

"Nipping along to see their shows. See if any of them use fog in their acts. See if any of them can disappear the way Foggy Jack did. All this fannying around with cups and balls – well, shall we say," he mocked Bigby's tone, "it ain't doing the trick."

Kipper left Scotland Yard feeling three feet taller. It was a rare occasion when he got one up on the smug bastard Bigby and his bleedin' pipe; he considered marking the day on his calendar.

***

Damien Deacus walked the puppet prostitute through the streets of Whitechapel, lurching and staggering to match her peculiar gait. His voice carried to Kipper's ears, which were stationed (along with the rest of the inspector) in a first floor window of *The Ferret's Legs*, where he was afforded a view of the main thoroughfare in both directions – provided the fog didn't congeal into a greasy peasouper. Already a thin mist hung in the air and the lampposts spilled yellowish pools around themselves. Piss clouds, thought Kipper, in rare poetic mood.

"Come on then, dearie," Deacus was encouraging his supposedly inebriated companion, "Let's have another chorus of *The Old Bull and Bush*. I'll be the old bull and you can be – the other one. Here, you ain't half a deadweight, girl, when you've got a drink or ten inside you."

Coppélia's head lolled; convincingly, Kipper thought. Or one of the springs in her neck was busted. Either way, Deacus was doing a bang-up job of getting the decoy to its agreed position. She was to be left at the mouth of an alley, in 'come hither' pose, and not to utter a word to potential clients until they had passed her by. Men of that inclination were accustomed to dollymops calling after them – it would all add to the illusion.

Kipper watched Deacus prop the puppet against a wall. He pawed and groped at her, making the requisite grunts and groans; anyone would think an ordinary transaction was under way but Kipper knew it was a cover. The lad was conducting final checks, a last-minute turning of the key in Coppélia's holes – Blimey, how much would a flesh-and-blood dollymop charge for that?

144

The lad stumbled away, whistling to himself and adjusting his trousers. Good lad, thought Kipper. Deacus had played his part well and as for Coppélia, she was artfully positioned to appear as though she belonged there. Even her blank stare suggested she was bored with her profession.

Now we wait; Kipper rubbed his hands in eager anticipation. He was looking forward to bettering smug bastard Bigby once and for all.

***

He did not have to wait for long. Within the hour, a figure emerged from the thickening mist, wearing the top hat and cloak Kipper was expecting to see. The man was dragging his right leg. If he's half lame, Kipper thought, he should be easier to nick.

On cue, Coppélia's mouth dropped open and she uttered an advertisement of her services, informing the passer-by that he could have access to her back passage for a tanner. At the sound of her strange, metallic voice, the figure froze and rotated on the spot. All Kipper could see was the man's silhouette, a darker shape within the pale grey fog. Coppélia's blonde wig was a dim blur of colour in the murk.

The man pounced. His hand went around the decoy dollymop's throat and he shoved her into the alley. Kipper swore. Fumbling in his pocket for his police whistle, he tore from the room and pelted down the stairs. The bar was crowded and Kipper's egress was impeded by the crowd of carousers having a singsong around a piano. Elbowed and shouldered off course, Kipper emitted swearwords and apologies in equal measure as beer was spilled and sloshed all over him. At last, he made his way to the street. A Hackney cab made him spring backwards as it appeared from nowhere and then seemed to take an age to trundle by.

Kipper crossed the street in prancing strides. Caution slowed him as he approached the alley mouth, the whistle in his fist

145

forgotten. Steeling himself lest horrors lay in wait, he stepped into the alley where the fog had failed to penetrate. The fog, he saw, was not the only one.

There was blood but not where Kipper expected. Coppélia's chin was dripping with it. Her head was tilted to one side; one eye was staring blankly while the other rolled around.

Something groaned. A shadow moved and groaned again.

"Who's there?" cried Kipper. "Police!"

The man was curled on the ground with his hands cupped on his crotch. His top hat was off, revealing golden curls of hair and a face red and sweating.

"Foggy Jack," said Kipper, pulling out a pair of handcuffs. "I am arresting you on suspicion of murder."

"Oh, don't be absurd!" snapped the man on the ground. He yelped in agony. "Arrest that woman. She damned near bit orf my tallywacker."

"She what?" said Kipper. He gave Coppélia a wary look and edged away from her. He stooped over the injured man. "What happened? Who are you?"

"I am Edward," the man winced through clenched teeth, "Lord Beighton. I was just taking my evening constitutional when I was assaulted by that – that creature."

"Oh, you was, was you?" said Kipper. "It's not what it looked like where I was standing."

Lord Beighton's mouth hung open as if he and Coppélia were of the same stock.

"Oh," he said. "Very well then, Inspector –?"

"Kipper," said Kipper.

"Really? Very well then, Inspector Kipper, I shall be pleased to relate to you the incident in vivid detail, provided you oblige me by summoning an ambulance. I really am in the most excruciating pain."

Twenty-Five

Well. That was a turn-up for this book! Who'd have thought it? That bleedin' toff, Lord Whatsisface – Beighton! Patronising prostitutes! Doling out dosh to dollymops!

I come running out of the Ferret's Legs and found Fishface trying to help the toff out of the alley. Let's get him to hospital, says the copper and I says No – on account of the new leg what Doctor Hoo had stuck on him – and I suggests we take him back to the gaff in Limehouse instead. The toff is all for it; he don't want to draw no attention to his shenanigans, I shouldn't wonder.

We gets a cab and all through the ride, the toff's protesting that the situation is not what it might look like. He says all this through grimaces of pain and I see we're going to have to tip the cabby extra for all the blood he's leaking on the upholstery.

"Oh, really?" says the copper and I can see he's a little bit amused by the toff's plight.

"I'm not Foggy Jack, damn you," spits the toff and his boat contorts in agony like a scrunched-up piece of paper.

"I can see that," says Kipper, "or you would have vanished long since."

"Eh?" winces the toff.

"You what?" says I.

"Scotland Yard," says Fishface and the words is dripping with contempt, "believes the killer to be a conjuror – a stage magician."

The toff sneers in derision.

"Well, he is dressed like one," I observes. "Stands to reason."

"The very idea!" the toff sneers. "A man of my standing! In show business!"

"A man of your standing was lying in an alley not long back," smirks the copper.

"And that is not how it appears," says the toff, with another reason to feel uncomfortable. "That woman! You must arrest her for common assault!"

The copper and me exchanges glances and we're both thinking the same thing: You can't arrest a puppet.

"If you must know," the toff would be blushing from top to toe, I'm sure, if he weren't so pale from the loss of blood, "I carry out a great deal of charitable work incognito."

"Where?" I says.

"In Whitechapel," he says slowly, as if I'm a bleedin' idiot. That's rich, coming from an actual rich, bleeding idiot. "I was merely offering that young lady succour."

"Ain't you got that backwards?" I interrupts. "Ain't she supposed to offer you that?"

The toff does his best to ignore me. His face is grey like a bedsheet what hasn't been changed for ages, and the sweat is pouring off of him. If it was me, I'd have sat back and saved my energy, but not him. He's keen to impress his innocence on us. "I was merely offering her funds for accommodation. A decent hotel where she could go and forsake the streets, even if only for one night."

Fishface purses his lips. "Got it all sorted, have you? Bridal suite at the Savoy?"

The toff blenches. "No!" he sounds scandalised. "I meant for her to go there alone. I am insulted to my core that you would infer—"

He swoons; he's on his way out. Just as well we're pulling up at Hoo's Limehouse warehouse. The doctor will sort him out and sharpish.

We – well, the copper does – pays off the cab and we bundle the toff into the warehouse and up to the lab. Doctor Hoo looks at us, all three, with cold eyes, then Hoo shoos the copper and me out of the lab and closes the door.

"He don't look too happy," says Fishface.

"He always looks like that," I shrugs – but I know this ain't strictly true. There's something else. Something else has got on Hoo's wick.

"Bloody hell," I smacks myself on the brow.

"What?" says Kipper.

"We've only bleedin' gone and forgot the dollymop, ain't we?"

The copper's jaw drops.

"He's put a lot of time and effort into her," I paces up and down and I chews at the skin at my thumbnail. "We've got to go back and fetch her."

"You can if you like," says Kipper, looking intently at the laboratory door. "Only I'm staying here to find out what else our flesh-and-blood friend has to say."

I stops pacing and pulls up a chair. The copper thinks it's for him but I sits on it; let him find his own bleedin' chair. Truth be told: I don't fancy facing that metal mistress on my Jack. I'd seen what she'd done to that toff. Well, I had a good idea but I thinks I'll sound out the copper.

"What do you reckon happened, then?" I nods at the door. He knows what I mean straight off.

"I reckon the posh git got a little bit too rough with her. I saw how he shoved her into that alley. That weren't no charitable donation he wanted to give her. I reckon he put himself in her mouth and she just about changed his religion for him, if you catch my meaning."

I crosses my legs. It don't bear thinking about.

"And all he can do is wallop her until she lets go. Before she can change him from lord to lady. Did you see how her head was out of whack?"

I nods. "Doctor Hoo's not going to be happy with us, getting his prize puppet beaten up."

"I don't give a rat's arsehole about that," says Kipper and now it's him what's pacing up and down. "All I know is I'm no closer to catching Foggy Jack."

"Perhaps your mates is right?" I offers but all I gets is a frown.

"Who?"

"Your mates down Scotland Yard. Perhaps he is a magician."

"They're not," he stamps his foot. "Not my mates and not right. Magician, my arse."

Before he can launch himself into a proper tirade, the lab door opens and Doctor Hoo is standing there with blood on his lab coat and dripping off of his gloves.

"Come in," he says.

He even bows his head.

***

In we went. The toff was lying spark out on a table, covered by a sheet up to his neck. The copper got to him first, a look of concern all over his mush, which the doctor interpreted faster than I could.

"He lives," said Doctor Hoo. "He rests."

"Well, ain't that a bleedin' relief," Fishface mopped at his brow with a handkerchief. "Only I don't want to think of the repercussions if he'd been killed by your contraption – and under my instructions!"

Typical copper, thought I. Covering his own back first. On the other hand, it was only a bleedin' toff we was talking about and a bleedin' arrogant one at that.

"Here," I said to Doctor Hoo, "What have you done to him?" I nodded at the sleeping pillock on the table, in particular his crotch region.

Before Hoo could speak, the toff sat up, bolt upright, with a gasp and a scream. He threw off the sheet, hopped off the table and ran around the lab like a cat with its Aristotle on fire. Well, I say 'ran' – his new leg was definitely in charge. The rest of him dragged behind it. Me and the copper watched in amusement and alarm but old Doctor Hoo, he just stood there – I've never known a doctor to be more patient, ha, ha! – until, after a few more laps, the toff tired himself out. Hoo injected something into the toff's arm. The toff swooned and fainted; me and the copper just about catched him in time and we heaved him back onto the table. I gathered up the sheet but the copper was pointing at the toff's privates – or rather, where his privates ought to be.

Instead of his tallywacker, there was another of Hoo's contraptions, like a little brass telescope.

"What the hell is that?" gasped Fishface.

"Improved model," said Doctor Hoo. And I could tell he was proud of his handiwork.

"You mean," I pointed at the device, "you've swapped his whatsit for a – whatever that is?"

"*Enhanced*," said Doctor Hoo with special emphasis. "Much better."

Inspector Kipper snatched the sheet and draped it over the toff. When the thing was hidden, the copper seemed more at ease. "I don't know what you've got going on here, Hoo," he lowered himself onto a chair, "And, frankly, I don't want to know. He's alive, so thanks for that; but if you can't help me catch Foggy Jack, the deal's orf." He looked directly at me. "Oh, don't worry; I'm not taking you back to the nick. I reckon you've got enough problems."

On the table, Lord Beighton stirred. He groaned a little and opened his eyes – it took him several attempts.

"I say," he said. "What have I been drinking? And may I have some more, what?" He laughed. He laughed alone. He looked from Hoo's stark face to mine, to the copper's and back again, and he appeared to remember something.

"Oh, no," he said quietly. "Oh, no; oh, no."

He lifted the sheet and peered beneath it at his naked, supposedly enhanced, body. He let the sheet fall then lifted it again, as if that would change the view.

"Good God, man!" he cried. "What have you done to me?"

"Improvement," said Doctor Hoo.

The toff looked aghast.

"Bigger," Hoo continued. "Longer. Faster. Harder."

The toff blenched. "Well, of course it's bloody harder – it's made of brass! What the bloody hell am I supposed to do with it?"

The copper got to his feet, looking like the world's weariest man. "Listen," he said. "I'm heading back to the nick. Leave you gentlemen to discuss the finer points of brass rubbing."

"You're a policeman!" the toff accused, reaching for Kipper's arm. "Arrest that man! Arrest both of them! What they've done to me – it's diabolical!"

Kipper sidestepped the toff's grasp. "I don't think they've dyed your bollocks at all." He looked to Hoo. "You haven't, have you?"

Hoo was inscrutable.

"Listen," Kipper looked the toff squarely in the eye. "These men saved your life so think about that before you start shouting the odds." He nodded to me and Hoo. "Gentlemen," he said and he headed for the door.

Twenty-Six

Kipper knew it was a mistake, trying to get one up on Bigby by recruiting that weirdo and his ne'er-do-well sidekick. What was I thinking, he scolded himself? He felt his way down the spiral staircase, descending into the inky gloom, bent on self-castigation rather than where he was going.

A loud crash brought him to the present. It was quickly followed by another. And a third. Kipper froze. It sounded like something heavy was being thrown against the outer door. Again and again until on the seventh or eighth try, the door yielded and someone (or something!) burst through it and entered the warehouse, leaving a fog-filled hole in its wake.

Behind and above Kipper, the lab door opened and Hoo and his assistant came out onto the landing, bearing lamps.

"What the bloody hell?" said Deacus.

"Ssh!" insisted Doctor Hoo.

"Is that you, Kipper?" Deacus trained his lamplight on the staircase. "Making all this bleedin' racket?"

"I can assure you it ain't!" Kipper whispered back. He climbed the stairs – there is safety in numbers after all. "Something's got in," he told them.

"Thing?" queried Hoo.

"Somebody then. I don't know; I didn't see it, did I?"

"Body?" queried Hoo.

"Some *one*, then. Bashed the bloody door in like it was made of paper."

Hoo and Deacus exchanged a glance.

"What?" said the inspector. He did not like the way the lamplight made gargoyles of their faces but he stepped closer to them all the same.

"I think we'd better shift ourselves," suggested Deacus.

"I tell you, one more bang like that and I just might."

"No, Inspector, I said 'shift' with an F."

Below, something moved in the stygian darkness. Something heavy. Dragging…

Kipper held his breath.

"It's coming for us!" gasped Deacus.

"The light," rumbled Doctor Hoo. He extinguished his lamp. Deacus moved to do the same but, panicked, Kipper made a grab for his lantern. They wrestled for a few seconds and the lamp flew from their clutches and sailed in a graceful arc over the stairwell, to land with a crash and an explosion of flame on the floor. The fire illuminated a shadowy figure; Kipper let out a yelp and scrambled for the laboratory door.

"Keep that thing away from me!" he cried, shouldering the door open.

The battered, contorted frame of Coppélia lunged for the staircase. Fire spread across the floor and errant flames nibbled at her wig and clothing.

"No," said Hoo.

"Sorry, boss," Deacus stammered, "Only we forgot about her, what with all the excitement. But she's back now so no harm done, eh?"

Fire glinted in the doctor's narrow eyes as he watched his creation stagger toward him.

"How?" he said.

That took Deacus by surprise. "What do you mean, 'How?'? I thought you'd made her do this. Given her some sort of homing instinct."

"Prostitute," said Hoo grimly. "Not pigeon."

Coppélia continued her climb, her head lolling like that of a hanged man. Her wig was completely ablaze, like a raging halo, and her clothes were dropping off her in cinders – not just her clothes, Deacus realised: her skin! The stench of burning hair and rubber and hot metal filled the air, overpowering even the smell of the smoke that was billowing below, as the conflagration engulfed the ground floor. Glass cracked and tinkled into pieces in the windows of the kitchen corner.

"This whole place is going up," said Deacus. "Better get a wiggle on."

But Doctor Hoo was transfixed. He stared at the approaching automaton until he was only inches from its fiery embrace. Deacus pulled him away and the arms closed around empty space. He bundled the doctor into the laboratory, where they found Kipper trying to get the toff to get dressed and get out.

Deacus slammed the door. Seconds later, Coppélia's fist came through it, splintering the wood into matchsticks.

"It's that – creature!" wailed Lord Beighton. "She's come to finish me orf – and not in the sexual way." He tried to station the inspector between himself and the monstrous apparition that was tearing is way into the room with apparently very little effort.

Hoo stood stock still, watching. His head shook but only slightly from side to side. No, no, no…

Deacus did his best to shepherd the toff and the copper to a window. "Look lively, gents," he urged. "For orf we must bugger and sharpish."

Smoke was rising between the floorboards and the heat of the inferno beneath was becoming unbearable. Deacus grabbed a stool and hurled it through the windowpane.

"Get out!" he instructed the others. He went back for Doctor Hoo, again yanking him free of the contraption's clutches at the last second. "Come on, Doctor! Time for us to go, mate!"

He pushed and bundled the doctor toward the window. The floor had begun to burn. Still, Coppélia kept coming, her hands reaching and grasping, her skeletal framework exposed in patches.

Deacus was dismayed to see Kipper and the toff still there. "Jump, you tits!"

"But – the river—" the toff protested.

"But – the fire!" Deacus mocked him.

It was the sight of the dollymop, hideously disfigured, that spurred Lord Beighton on. He tossed himself out of the broken window and dropped out of sight. A splash followed his disappearance.

"Go on, then," Deacus nodded at the inspector. "Out you go."

"No; after you," said Kipper.

"After you! Listen, we ain't got time for social niceties. Get out the pissing window, will you?"

Kipper bristled but did as he was told.

After the splash, Deacus dragged the doctor to the window. "Come on; snap out of it, Doctor." He grunted. The doctor would not budge. He extended a hand toward Coppélia's. Their fingertips were barely an inch apart.

"Oh, no, you don't!" Deacus intervened. He kicked the dollymop in her belly, knocking her backwards, then he head-butted Hoo in his and rushed him to the open window, the night sky and the fresh air.

As they plummeted to the river, the warehouse collapsed in on itself. Flames stretched for the heavens, their ravenous crackles like demonic laughter. Orange and gold shone across the water like spilled paint. Four heads bobbed on the surface, watching the building burn.

"I say!" gasped Lord Beighton. "That's put a stop to her, what!"

"Not exactly," said Kipper. "Look!"

From the toppling structure, a flaming figure swan dived into the river.

"Gawd help us," Kipper murmured.

The men scrambled to the shore with Kipper assisting the toff and Deacus having to drag Doctor Hoo along with him. They watched and waited on the mud bank, scanning the water for signs.

"What the bloody hell is that thing?" said Lord Beighton. "It's like a thing possessed."

Doctor Hoo turned his head. "Repeat!"

"What?" the toff blinked. "All I said was she's like a thing possessed."

Hoo nodded slowly.

"What?" said Deacus. "What?"

But Hoo did not respond.

"Oh, Gawd!" cried Kipper, pointing frantically. "Here she comes!"

An arm broke the surface, rippling the reflections of the blaze. With dogged determination, Coppélia crawled out onto the shore. Her insides, most of them visible, popped and twanged as she dragged herself by the hands out of the water and toward the men, all of whom were standing agog. All bar one, that is, for Doctor Hoo approached the relentless robot. He raised his foot and brought his boot heel down sharply on the automaton's neck. Coppélia came to a sudden and total stop.

"Coo," said Deacus. "She weren't giving up, was she?"

"Good lord," said the toff. "Perhaps she couldn't get enough of me, what!" He essayed a laugh; no one joined in.

Inspector Kipper gave the creature's body a tentative prod with his toe. "Quite dead, is she?"

"Never alive," said Hoo.

"That's not what I asked."

"Here," said Deacus. "Wasn't you storming off in a huff or something? You wanted no more to do with us, if you recall."

"What?" said Kipper. "Oh, yes. My grand exit was waylaid by that thing. Damned right I want no more to do with you. Goodnight, *gentlemen* – for want of a better word."

He picked his way across the mud and detritus, his clothes

dripping and his shoes squelching, heading for a jetty that would take him to the dock road.

Hoo, Deacus and Lord Beighton watched him go, but a strange voice called him back.

"Don't go, Inspector!"

The men were alarmed to find the voice was coming from the almost-severed head of Coppélia. One eye faced upwards, rolling at the sky. Kipper stopped in his tracks and, with a chill in the very marrow of his bones, turned slowly around.

"Please don't go," the shrill voice implored. "It's me, ain't it? Your old mucker."

"Sprite?" Kipper gasped.

"Got it in one." The lone eye winked.

Twenty-Seven

Well! Nobody weren't expecting that! I can say that without fear of contradiction. I could tell by the look on Hoo's boat that he hadn't told her to say none of those words. He was as surprised as the rest of us. That copper, he stopped in his tracks and all, and he came back, squelching across the mud to get a closer look. The toff's eyes were large as plates – dinner plates, I mean, not feet – and he was trying to edge behind the doctor for safety.

"Hoi," says the voice. "Get me on my plates again, will you? Only it ain't too dignified lying in the dirt. It's all right – the water's put the fire out."

We hesitated a bit but Hoo nodded so the copper and me we lifted the damaged dollymop from the mud and tried to stand her upright.

"Hello, again, Inspector," the eye rolled around to Fishface. "Nice to see you again."

"Ho, ho!" the toff chuckled. "Sounds like the inspector's been dipping his wick, what!"

I don't know who looked the more insulted, the copper or the lopsided dollymop.

"You know her?" said Doctor Hoo, placing a hand on the copper's shoulder.

"I bloody don't!" said the copper. "I mean, we have met. Under different circumstances, of course."

"Explain," said Hoo.

"Yeah," I chimed in. I was keen to hear this and all.

"No," said Coppélia – or rather, whoever was speaking through her. "I think I'd better do the talking. I have a lot to say. But let's get

159

indoors, shall we? I don't like standing out here with the damp air whistling round me Aris."

***

Where could we take her? The warehouse weren't nothing but a smouldering bonfire. Hoo said 'Harley Street' so it fell to me to try to find us a cab. 'Make it two,' said the toff. He said he'd had enough adventure for one night and was going back to his gaff on Grosvenor Square, and I said couldn't we all go there instead? But he weren't having none of it and as soon as the first Hansom shows up, he jumps in without a by-your-leave and orf he buggers.

"Ain't that bleedin' charming," muttered this Sprite person, speaking through the dollymop.

"Who are you? What are you?" I arsked. Reasonable questions, I'm sure you'll agree.

"Not out here," Sprite urged. She'd got both eyes working together now, and they shifted from side to side as if she suspected someone was about and earwigging.

She kept her lip buttoned in the cab and all the way across town. It was only when we was in Hoo's Harley Street office with the doors and windows closed and the curtains drawn that she seemed to relax. Hark at me – going on like she was a real person – but there was something about her. Like when you watch a puppet show – and who don't love a puppet show? – and you forgets they ain't real. You forget they're on strings or they've got somebody's hand up them. Well, this Sprite was working Coppélia so well, all sorts of expressions danced across her boat, and the way she moved and all. She was wearing the dollymop like a costume, I suppose you might say. Well, you don't have to, on account of I've just said it.

The four of us sat in a ring of chairs in Hoo's office with a candle on the floor between us. Giant, shadowy copies of ourselves reached up the walls to the ceiling. It wasn't half eerie, I can tell you, but that was nothing compared to what come next. Here's what that Sprite told us and it's a tale and a half and no mistake.

***

My name is lost, forgotten as the language of my people is forgotten. You know me as 'Sprite' for that is the closest approximation in your tongue of what I am. I was here, on this island, long before your kind arrived. Long before the trees, even. Long before anything but the elements, the wind and rain.

We were free then, my people, to roam or settle as we chose. But then, you came. In boats you came and claimed these islands as your own. Imagine the land as a map; you spread across it like a stain across paper. But we accommodated you, despite the ravages you visited on the land. Had we known you would bring him *with you, your presence would not have been tolerated.*

He – you call him Foggy Jack, as though he is a pet or favourite! He is born of the evil that men do. Murders, wars, and all the ill-feeling man has for his fellow man. You brought all of that to these peaceful isles where it found something in the air, perhaps, or the wind and rain, that gave it independence.

He feeds on your animosity. In London, your largest settlement, at its largest to date, he has made his home. Here is misery, poverty and disease. Want and ignorance. Depravity and greed. Nourished by the evil that men do, he roams, he thrives. But the more he wallows in the cruelty of man, the more he wants. London will not be enough to contain him. He wants to spread his wings until they encompass the world.

But what of the killings? The murders of the women that have brought him to your notice. You may think he is spreading fear – I believe he rather celebrates it! Each killing is an offering, a votive thank-you to the elements. But here is the key, gentlemen: he has to kill if he is to maintain his presence in the physical world. Bloodshed is his anchor. It cleaves him to the city, gives him form, gives him purpose.

I know this because I use a similar method. You will recall, Inspector, before my present predicament, I was mired in mud and dirt. Like any of the thousands of urchins that crawl through the streets like ants. That filth kept me grounded so I was able to be present, to interact – for I do enjoy conversing with your kind – but also it kept me hidden from him. He has been a scourge of my people, devouring them, absorbing their energy to augment his own. I fear I am the last of my kind.

But that is not the most important reason why he must be stopped. You cannot let your world fall to him. You must not allow his noxious fog to cloak the planet in evil.

To do this you must destroy me. This form I occupy – a remarkable contrivance, Doctor; you are a clever man – this form must be dismantled, for you have unwittingly created the means by which Foggy Jack may travel, murdering as he goes. He will anchor himself to this metal body with the blood of his victims – just as I am bound to it by the blood of that fool who accosted me – and his terror will spread, and men will be encouraged to plumb deeper depths of cruelty, inflicting atrocities on each other, until all are dead and the world a poisoned playground.

So I shed my urchin form to bring this device back to you for disposal. What will become of me, I cannot say. Perhaps I will survive the dismantling. Perhaps some friendly breeze will carry me to a mud bank where I can fashion myself an urchin form once more.

You look pale, gentlemen. I have spoken of things beyond your ken. I beg you, do not dwell, do not dispute, but act! Act quickly to bring an end to Foggy Jack. Or face the ruin of everything.

***

Bloody hell.

Twenty-Eight

Kipper threw back his head and covered his face with his hands. Sprite's tale swirled in his head. It was fantastical and as easy to grasp as – as fog.

"Talk about your bedtime stories," muttered Deacus.

Doctor Hoo said nothing. He looked at his creation, now still, its eyes as vacant as any doll's. He pulled a tool from his pocket, a long, thin screwdriver, but he could not bring himself to use it.

"Put that away," said Kipper. "You're not going to touch her."

"What?" said Deacus. "You heard what she said. We've got to take her to pieces and then burn them or bury them – or both!"

"No," Kipper got to his feet. "If what she said is true – and I can't believe I'm thinking that it is – then this is our best and only chance."

"Chance for what?"

"You heard her. This puppet is what he wants. A means to travel the world. What better bait could we have? Eh?"

"No!" cried Deacus.

Kipper ignored him. "Doctor, can you make some modifications to Coppélia? Some adjustments to her workings, so that control of her movements is not her own?"

Doctor Hoo gave a slow nod.

"Don't you see?" Kipper rounded on Deacus. "We get him in there, then we march him off somewhere."

"Sorry to break this to you but I don't think Bow Street nick is going to hold him."

"Not there! Think – there must be somewhere – somewhere in London we can send him. Wall him in so he never gets out."

"It's a headscratcher and no mistake."

"That's right," Kipper's face was grim. "There can be no mistake. Doctor, get to work. Deacus, you're with me."

"Where we going?"

"A tour of the city. There must be somewhere we can stash him."

"You think this is going to be easy, don't you, Kipper?"

"No," said Kipper. "It's going to be as easy as herding cats, I reckon."

"No," said Doctor Hoo. "Trapping fog."

***

"Here," said Deacus as their cab pulled up. "I thought you weren't taking me back to the nick."

"I'm not," said Kipper. "I need to see Sergeant Adams about – Why am I telling you this?"

Deacus grinned. "We're in this together, ain't we?"

Kipper shivered. But he did not contradict – he couldn't. How your priorities change, he reflected! Only a few hours ago, what had been driving him was the desire to get one over on Bigby and the rest of Scotland Yard. And now – now, well, he didn't know exactly what he was embroiled in but one thing was sure: Foggy Jack had to go.

"You look pale, Inspector. Here, don't he look pale?"

"Not half," said Sergeant Adams, who had come out to intercept the inspector. "I done some digging, sir." He presented a sheaf of papers. "About our doctor friend."

"Oh?" Kipper accepted the bundle.

"Oh?" said Deacus, getting out of the carriage. Kipper tucked the papers under his arm protectively.

"Good man, Adams," he nodded. "But what I need right now is some kind of a – a what-do-you-call-it, a gazetteer?"

"A map?" suggested Deacus.

"An almanac," Adams nodded. "I've got one inside. Everything that's worth knowing about London is in it, and a few things what ain't."

"Good man," Kipper followed him inside. Deacus hurried after and arrived in time to see the sergeant take out a fat little book from under his desk. He handed it to the inspector. Kipper began to thumb through it.

"There's an index at the back," Adams advised.

"I know!" snapped Kipper. "What I'm after…"

"Where's the deepest place in London?" said Deacus.

"This is police business," said Kipper.

Sergeant Adams rubbed his chin. The beard was merely a shadow of its former self. "I'd have to say… Perhaps the dungeons. Up at the Tower."

Deacus nodded. "Could be."

"Tower of London…" Kipper ran his finger down the alphabetical list of contents.

"Or…"

Adams and Deacus looked at each other with wide eyes as the same thought occurred to them at the same instant.

"The Underground!" they said in unison.

"Well, of course they're underground," said Kipper. "They're dungeons."

"No, sir. The trains, sir! You know: them what goes under the ground."

Kipper glared at them both. "Yes, I know what underground trains are! What about them?"

"They're digging new tunnels all the time," said Deacus. "Running in all directions. Whole city is turning into a rabbit warren."

"I'm not sure I likes it, sir," said Adams. "People going underground in one place and then popping up in another. Makes it hard for us to chase them, sir."

"On the other hand, it gets the criminals off the streets," said Deacus with a wink.

Kipper was at a loss. "I don't get it…"

"The tunnels, sir. They all run at different depths, sir, otherwise the trains'd all collide, sir."

"So?"

"Think about it, sir. Which is the deepest tunnel?"

"Stands to reason," said Deacus.

Kipper leafed through the almanac. "Bah, this thing is out of date!" He thrust the book at Adams's chest. "Find out where the deepest tunnel is. I'm orf to Scotland Yard. Deacus, with me."

He turned on his heels and strode from the nick. Deacus and Adams shared a what-can-you-do look.

***

"So what's at Scotland Yard?" Deacus settled back into his seat in the cab.

"I'm hoping a bunch of magicians," said Kipper. His feet tapped the floor – there wasn't room in the carriage for pacing. He chewed his lower lip as an aid to thinking.

"You're going to put on a show?"

"Something like that." He remembered the sheaf of papers under his arm. He untied the string.

"Give's a look," said Deacus.

"Police business," said Kipper.

"Ain't I up to my neck in police business? Besides, he's my employer. Perhaps I can shed some light on what's written there."

"Like what?"

"Well, I don't know until I read it, do I?"

Kipper exhaled. "I suppose not. You can have each page after I've read it. You can read, can't you?"

"Course I can!" Deacus was affronted. "He taught me, didn't he?"

"Who did?"

"Yes."

As in all things, Sergeant Adams had been very thorough in compiling a dossier on Doctor Hoo. Most of it consisted of articles from newspapers, stamped PROPERTY OF BRITISH LIBRARY – How Adams had acquired them, Kipper did not want to know. There was also a couple of flyers advertising a travelling circus on which Hoo was billed as a 'novelty act'. Kipper handed these directly to Deacus.

"Memories," said Deacus. "I met him at the circus, you know."

"Is it pertinent?"

"It was to me. He made wonderful things. Toys. Clockwork toys. He had a flea circus. Beautiful, it was. You could almost imagine the little things jumping on the trampoline, or walking the tightrope. So clever."

"Oh, yeah?"

"Yeah!" Deacus's jaw dropped. "He's been perfecting his work ever since. You saw Coppélia. When she was first made. Beautiful piece of work."

"That's one way of looking at it," said Kipper with a sniff. His attention was caught by the next paper in the bundle. "Oho!" he exclaimed. "Turns out your Doctor Hoo ain't who he says he is." He proffered a yellowed newspaper clipping.

"Is any of us?" said Deacus.

"This ain't no time for depth," said Kipper. "Have a butcher's at what it says there. Read it with your own mince pies."

Deacus's mince pies narrowed. "Here, are you taking the gypsy's?"

Kipper didn't answer. He poked the headline:

BROUHAHA AT DOCTORS' DINNER

In narrow columns, dense and tiny print detailed the occasion when the Lord Mayor's annual function for the medical profession was cut short and the police had to be brought in. Deacus squinted in the dim light and read out loud.

"…The hullabaloo was instigated by the arrival of discredited medic, Doctor Montgomery Hood, who had infiltrated the evening's entertainment, the Angels of Arcady, a singing troupe from Walthamstow. Hood, forty-three, approached His Worship's table and demanded a hearing. Readers will recall our coverage of Hood's dismissal from the profession six months ago under a cloud of rumour. Unnatural practices and devil worship—

"Here," Deacus looked up. "What's all this? This ain't about Doctor Hoo. This bloke's name is Hood, with a D on the end. And look at the date. This article come out fifty years ago and this Hood geezer was forty-three back then. Does Doctor Hoo look like a bloke what's in his nineties? And here, where it says there was a fire…"

Kipper frowned and peered at the paper. "Witnesses gazed on in horror as Hood was engulfed by flames from an oil lamp dashed at his feet by hands unknown…"

"I arsk you," said Deacus indignantly. "That ain't Hoo. Your sergeant's leading you up the bleedin' path, if you arsks me."

Kipper took back the clipping and returned it to the bundle. "Well," he said. "We'll see."

"We bleedin' well will," said Deacus. He folded his arms in defiance.

They spent the rest of the ride to Great Scotland Yard in disagreeable silence. Deacus whistled when he saw the building – much to Kipper's annoyance. The rear entrance on the thoroughfare that gave the station its name had become the main access point and was bustling with people coming and going through the wide green doors with a purposeful air.

"Stone me," breathed Deacus.

"Not allowed," Kipper muttered darkly.

"Look at the size of this place. Makes your nick down Bow Street look like an apple cart."

Kipper grunted. "Any comparisons with Piccadilly Circus will not be received favourably." They went in.

A constable with impressive mutton chops greeted them at the front desk. "Hello."

"Hello," said Deacus.

"Hello," said Kipper. "Tell Bigby I want to see him."

The constable looked him up and down. "Oh, you do, do you?"

Deacus intervened. "Here, show some respect! This is only Kipper of Bow Street you've got here."

The constable was nonplussed; the name meant nothing to him.

"Blimey," Deacus shook his head. "Do they let anybody work here or only the thick ones?"

The constable thought about this and reached for his truncheon. Deacus nipped behind the inspector. Kipper flashed his warrant card. The constable quailed.

"Spot of palaver, eh?" Bigby appeared through a cloud of pipe smoke. "Hello, Johnny!" He pumped Kipper's hand and caught sight of Deacus. "I see. Up to his old tricks again, is he?"

"I am not!" Deacus protested.

"New tricks, then, what!" Bigby laughed. "Come through to my office for a cup of tea and a chinwag. Worrall?"

"Sir!" the constable stood to attention.

"Rustle up some tea; there's a good man."

Constable Worrall blinked but did not move. Bigby ushered his visitors around the desk and into a corridor.

"Don't expect much in the way of tea," he warned. "Constable Worrall's harmless enough but he's no Sergeant Adams. Seriously considering poaching him from you, Johnny, so watch out."

Kipper bristled.

Bigby steered them into an office that was like Kipper's in name alone. Bigby's office was furnished like a comfortable living room or gentleman's study. Sofas and potted plants vied for space among the bookshelves and cabinets. Deacus was visibly impressed – and so was Kipper, if the angry pursing of his lips was any indication.

"Sorry about the mess," Bigby waved dismissively at the spotless room. "Bit chaotic and everything, what with the move and all."

"Move?" said Kipper.

"Haven't you heard?" Bigby smirked. "They're giving us a spanking new building. In Victoria. Isn't that marvellous?"

"Bleedin' marvellous," said Kipper. He declined the invitation to take a seat.

"Now what can I do for you, Johnny? My guess is a man of your dedicated approach isn't here for social reasons, good though it is to see you." He nodded to Deacus. "Want me to interrogate this one for you? Give him the treatment?"

Deacus paled to think what the treatment might entail.

"No, ta," said Kipper. "He's with me. But there's one thing you can help me with, if you'd be so kind."

"Of course. Name it."

"Them magicians you brung in for questioning," said Kipper. "Still got them?"

Twenty-Nine

You know when you lights a gas lamp and it flares up bright before it settles down? Well, that was what Inspector Fishface was like – that same flare was in his eyes but he weren't showing no signs of settling down. Something was driving him, keeping him going – something like madness I shouldn't be surprised. He'd got the bit between his teeth all right and he weren't letting go of it until Foggy Jack was stopped.

He kept me on board; I suppose he wanted to keep Doctor Hoo sweet (I can't get used to thinking of him as Doctor Hood – and I certainly wasn't going to call him that to his face. I'll leave them worms in their can for now). Fishface had got Hoo working on Coppélia to restore her to her former glory, only now she had that Sprite thing living inside her so I suppose for him, for Doctor Hoo, it was almost like he'd got a proper patient again. So, Fishface was keeping me apprised of his plan but he got me under strict instructions not to tell a soul a word of it and he certainly weren't sharing it with his mates from Scotland Yard. He'd got a right bee in his bonnet about that lot. Professional jealousy or something. And he didn't half give that Sergeant Adams a hard time about keeping the place tidy. He kept shouting out for antimacassars and doilies and what-not.

Anyway, the plan involved luring Foggy Jack away from Whitechapel and up to Hampstead Heath. Sprite said Foggy Jack would be weaker there, away from the sites of his murders, so he'd be keen to shed some blood there to anchor himself. How was he going to pull this off? How was Kipper going to entice the killer away from his usual haunts? It seems daft to spell it out but, like

I said, Kipper was driven. He was either a bleedin' genius or a madman or a bit of both, I shouldn't wonder.

He got them magicians what Scotland Yard had rounded up and he took them back to Bow Street nick. He asked them to show him how they might make themselves disappear – he wanted to learn the trick of it and use it in his plan – but of course, they wouldn't say a dicky bird, on account of their secret professional code or something – so he said he'd lock them all up as accessories to murder or something, which really got their backs up on account of them being keen to get back to work, performing shows to put bread on the table and then make it disappear again. So I piped up and said if they weren't going to show him how to do it, they'd have to do it themselves. Kipper shoved me aside and arsked what did I think I was playing at and I said he ought to recruit the lot of them as special constables or something. The magicians heard this and arsked if they'd be paid for their trouble and Kipper snarled at them like he was a bulldog and they was a bunch of cats who'd climbed into his yard. I gave him a nudge and said it was only right and proper they should be paid for their performance and he said he'd see what he could do.

So, they was all on board and we was all poring over a map, showing the route from Whitechapel to the Heath and Kipper was marking it with little crosses and telling each magician which was his spot. I was sent around all the pubs on the route to get the word out to all the dollymops what worked that patch to keep a low profile, which didn't take much doing because most of them was already avoiding Whitechapel like the bleedin' plague on account of them wanting to keep their insides where they was.

It all seemed to be going quite well and we was almost ready for the orf, when Sergeant Adams came into the office, only this time it wasn't to wield his feather duster.

"Sir!" he said and his face was all pale. He had decided not to grow his beard back, it looked like. "There's been another one."

172

Kipper swore and thumped the table. "Men," he cast a look around at me and the magicians. "This just makes it all the more imperative that we catch this bastard."

"Oh, no!" Sergeant Adams interjected before Fishface could launch himself into a stirring speech to fire us all up. "There's no need to catch the bastard, sir."

We all looked at him like he had gone out.

"On account of he's already here," Adams explained. "He's only bleedin' gone and turned himself in."

***

Oh, the consternation and confusion that caused! Kipper couldn't get to the door fast enough and he trampled the toes of several magicians on his way out. I followed, only I was more polite and apologetic as I shoved and trampled, because manners don't cost nothing.

Kipper yanks open the door to the interrogation room and I looks over his shoulder, half-expecting the room to be full of fog. There was a bloke sitting at the table. He was wearing a top hat and cloak but his head was bowed. He was staring at his gloves – at first I thought he was wearing red gloves but then I realised they was white, or had been to start with, only now they was drenched in blood. Kipper stepped in and I edged my way in behind him. It was a dangerous thing to do, getting into an enclosed space with a violent killer and especially one what had supernatural powers and all.

"...Jack?" ventured Kipper, for want of anything else to call him.

"I'm afraid not," said the bloke and he lifted his head. I let out a gasp, on account of it weren't Foggy Jack sat sitting there but a boat I recognised all too well. He didn't half look mournful as he looked from the inspector's eyes to mine. It was him, wasn't it?

Edward, Lord bleedin' Beighton.

***

173

He let out a roar like a lion what's had its tail trodden on and he lunged himself at me. "This is your fault! You and that doctor!" he said, in-between the shouts and the curses. His cloak fell open and I saw that the white of his shirt and weskit was all red and his trousers was all wet. Blood, of course. Well, the inspector was quick off the mark. Him and a couple of bobbies grabbed hold of Beighton and forced him back to his chair.

"You'd better go," Kipper said to me but to our surprise it was Beighton what spoke against this suggestion.

"No," he said, calmly but his breath was heavy. "Let him stay. He needs to hear this."

"You've got a brass neck," said Kipper.

"I don't think it's his neck we need to worry about," I said.

Lord Beighton looked at me. "I am sorry," he said. "Please, sit down." He said it with that easy grace that toffs have sometimes, as if he was inviting me to take tea in his bleedin' parlour. So, we sits down, the inspector and me, across the table from the toff. He's made quite a mess of the table top already; there's blood pooling, dripping from his cuffs. I tried not to look at it but it turned out to be better than looking into his woebegone eyes as he told us his tale.

"A man – even a gentleman," he began, having to clear a lump in his throat, "– has… needs. And such needs may be met quite readily on the streets of a city like London. One does not have to go far or look too hard. In Whitechapel, one may meet a certain type of, ah, businesswoman, who—"

"Bloody hell," Kipper interrupted. "We're going to get nowhere if you're going to beat around the bush like this. Just tell us what happened and speak as plainly as you can. We're all men of the world here."

"Very well," said Beighton, steeling himself. "I went looking for a shag – it's something I have done from time to time; I'm not proud of it but I'm not ashamed either. If one has the money, why not?"

It was Kipper's turn to clear his throat. It brought His Lordship up sharp.

"I digress," he admitted. "I shall endeavour to stick to the facts. I found a young lady – I use the term loosely – and after brief negotiation of, ah, activity and price, we entered an alley between the pub and the fire station."

I nodded. I knew the place – not the young lady, I hasten to add.

"I asked her to perform certain proofs – I needed to know she was a real, flesh-and-blood dollymop and not one of the Doctor's automata. Once bitten, and all that, what!"

He laughed grimly. We didn't.

"So I gave her a thorough inspection; she was the genuine article, all right and, in the process I found myself becoming thoroughly aroused. The new, ah, appendage the Doctor had fitted, rose to the occasion, shall we say? I was eager, of course, to try it out. But when, she, ah," he squirmed, "put her hand into my undergarments, her eyes grew wide with horror. 'It ain't half cold,' she observed, backing away. I should have – would have let her go – but by then it was too late. The, ah, device was activated and there was no going back. It was as though the thing had a mind of its own. It telescoped from my clothing and began to whirr and rotate, snaking its way toward the dollymop's nether regions. She was backed against a wall, you understand; I was blocking her egress."

"Dirty bastard!" I breathed until Kipper told me what that meant.

It was becoming harder – I should say 'more difficult' – for His Lordship to get his words out. We was getting to the nitty-gritty of the incident. I could see he was horrified and sickened by what he had done.

"I couldn't stop it; you must believe that!" his eyes were wild and desperate. "You've seen how my leg can run away with me? It's the same with this – this thing! Once it was activated, there was no stopping it. It was hell-bent on having its way. *Run,* I told the girl, but there was nowhere for her to go. The thing would not let her pass. I tried to leave the alley but it pulled me back in as though I was magnetised. The power of the thing was more than I could withstand. Look at my hands; see how I clawed at the walls, trying to find purchase, trying to hold on so the girl could make good her escape – but the thing was relentless.

"And then it – it entered her, pounding repeatedly like some sort of piston. She screamed and I thought someone would come and tear me away from her, but no one did. Then she passed out. Still the thing would not stop and – and – then…"

He looked pale and sickly; he was sweating like a chunk of cheese what's got the flu.

"Go on!" Kipper urged.

"And then – it opened her up. Like a can opener – you are familiar with such a device? It – what did the Bard say? – unseamed her from the nave to the chops. The gore was flying everywhere. I am drenched in it, as you can see. Please, I beg you, let me get out of these contaminated clothes. I know that I cannot scrub the stain from my soul. What I have done is indelibly marked on my conscience. But please, let me try to get even the smallest comfort, I—"

He broke down completely then. Huge, wracking sobs shook his body. I couldn't help feeling sorry for him. And perhaps he was right. Perhaps Doctor Hoo was partly to blame for that dollymop's demise. I don't know; perhaps the man what sells the gun is as guilty as him what shoots somebody with it.

Inspector Kipper got to his feet. He was a little shaky on his pins and, I must confess, so was I, having heard the gruesome details. We left him there, sobbing and broken. I heard the inspector whisper to Sergeant Adams to take him in some blankets and a bucket of water.

"Bloody hell…" said Kipper. "What a mess!"

"Poor bastard," I nodded in the direction of the interview room. "How's he going to live with himself after all that?"

Kipper shook his head. He had about as many answers as I did – which is to say, not a bleedin' one.

"We must press on with the plan," he said, straightening his spine. That glint, that spark of obsession was back in his minces again. "After this incident, the dollymops'll clear out of Whitechapel, making it easier for us to lure Foggy Jack away to Hampstead Heath…"

"Oh, you reckon, do you?"

"I do," he said. "We carry on. You make sure the Doctor is ready with our metal friend at the end of the line, and I'll make sure Foggy Jack gets there."

He could probably tell from the look on my boat that I was less than convinced. He clapped his hand on me shoulder.

"It will work," he said, with his chin jutting out with determination. "It bleedin' well has to."

Thirty

Sergeant Adams professed his keenness to take part. Kipper was loath to put him in the firing line. What if Foggy Jack recognises you, he asked? Adams shrugged and said he'd wear a different colour syrup and a completely new outfit. You need somebody reliable for the last leg, he told the inspector, somebody to deliver the killer to the last stop on the line. Adams didn't think the magicians, who had been pressganged into service, would be able to pull it off.

"What about Scotland Yard?" he asked, risking the wrath of his superior.

Kipper treated the suggestion with scorn. "They're too busy getting ready to move house," he sneered. "Besides which, they can't do the disappearing trick – although I wish they bloody well would."

Deacus pored over the map. "We get one chance at this," he said. "I ain't confident."

"You don't have to be," said Kipper. "You just get Doctor Hoo there and then keep your head down."

"We don't know what we're dealing with."

"Which is why I need you to talk to that Sprite creature. Anything she can tell us about Foggy Jack, you can relay back to me. I've got magicians to drill."

Deacus grinned.

"What?" Kipper frowned.

"You need me! The coppers need me!"

"Desperate times," said Kipper. "One false move…"

"One false move and we're all in the shit."

"Not half," said Kipper. "Sergeant Adams will sort you out a cab."

***

In the yard behind Bow Street nick, a dozen stage magicians shifted uncomfortably in their new attire. Sergeant Adams walked along the line, carrying out an inspection and making minor adjustments, prior to Inspector Kipper giving them the onceover.

"Here," said one, who operated under the stage name of Amazo the Amazing. "It don't feel right being stood here with no trousers on."

"But you've got lovely legs," teased Adams. "Put on an extra petticoat if you're feeling the cold. And you – Startling Boffo – get a shave, will you?"

Startling Boffo looked scandalised. "My legs?"

"I was thinking more of the handlebar moustache."

"But it's my pride and joy! It's my trademark."

"I thought your trademark was being shit," said Amazo, deriving laughter from the others.

Startling Boffo waved his fist. "Come here and say that."

"Gentlemen, gentlemen!" Sergeant Adams intervened. "Let's keep things civil, shall we? Comport ourselves like ladies? Which brings us to the next part. The way we walk. Observe."

He paraded from one end of the yard to the other, sashaying and mincing as though wearing heels. The magicians wolf-whistled and catcalled and made suggestive remarks.

"Of course," said Adams, "It ain't the same with me uniform on. But give it a go. Not too much, mind. Keep it real. You've got to advertise your wares while at the same time looking raddled and jaded as though you've been on the streets for donkey's. Mickey Marvel, you first."

Mickey Marvel, a tall, gangling fellow, was reluctant at first. His peers giggled and jeered as Mickey tottered a few steps, with one hand on his hip and the other on his breastbone.

"Hoi, Mickey. How much, darlin'?"

"Here, Mickey. How much for the back door?"

Sergeant Adams waved at them to shut up. It was too much for Mickey Marvel. He returned to the line and put his shawl over his head. The others brayed their ridicule.

"Gentlemen!" Sergeant Adams roared. "You are forgetting the grave circumstances, the serious reasons behind this charade. And if that ain't enough for you to make an effort, look at it like this: you're being paid, gentlemen, to put on a performance. See these skirts, these blouses and shawls as your costume – your work clothes, gentlemen. You're playing to an audience of one and this geezer, if he don't like the show, well, he won't just chuck a few rotten tomatoes, if you get my meaning. You've got to convince him, if only for a couple of seconds, that you are the real deal. Or you could end up wearing your insides on your outsides. So start strutting, fellows; start selling yourselves. Get ready to put on the show of your lives!"

Half an hour later, Inspector Kipper went out into the yard to find twelve prancing prostitutes, parading up and down. Some leaned against walls in provocative poses. Others looked him up and down and winked lasciviously. Kipper scoured the painted faces.

"Adams? Which is Sergeant Adams?"

"Here, sir!"

Kipper turned to find a vision of commercial femininity before him. Adams was sporting a black wig, piled high. Paste earrings dangled like chandeliers. A sapphire brooch winked at his collarbone. His outfit of velvet and lace was elegantly cut. He peered at the inspector through a lorgnette.

"Shag me!" Kipper gasped.

"It'll cost you," said Adams.

"No, what I mean is, what are you like? All tarted up like minor royalty or something."

"I thought I'd go high end," said Adams.

"I bet that costs more," jeered Startling Boffo.

"High class, I mean," Adams glared at him. "He don't just go after the gutter trade, you know."

Kipper nodded; Adams had a point. "I think you're enjoying this a bit too much. My concern is, can you run in that skirt?"

"Let's hope we don't have to find out," said Adams.

"Right, you lovely lot," Kipper clapped his hands. "Let's see you disappear."

Thirty-One

I didn't like it. I didn't like it one little bit. What was I doing, caught up in police operations? I should rather be legging it out of the city and lying low for a while until it all blew over. Let them catch Foggy Jack on their own! But, of course, he had a hold over me, didn't he, that Inspector Kipper? If I didn't cooperate, he'd bang me up again. My liberty in exchange for Doctor Hoo's help – that was the deal. I could do it now, do a runner and never look back – only of course I couldn't, on account of I couldn't let Doctor Hoo down, could I? Not after all he's done for me, not after all what we've been through together.

So I went back to the gaff on Harley Street where he was repairing Coppélia, who was to play an important role in proceedings – or rather, it was that Sprite creature living inside of her that was the important one – I don't really know no more. All this talk about sprites and mechanical dollymops and killers what was made out of fog, I arsk you! Not your everyday experience, is it? Well, it might be yours, I don't know, do I?

Hoo didn't look pleased to see me. Well, I wasn't expecting him to turn cartwheels, but then on the other hand he didn't try to strangle me neither, so I'll give him the benefit of the doubt and say he didn't mind me being there.

"Hello, Damien!" said the voice from inside Coppélia, without moving her mouth, which I thought was a bit creepy.

"Hello, ah, Sprite," I nodded, trying not to stare. "How's tricks?"

"That's rather a question you should arsk the magicians, ain't it?" Sprite shot back and laughed. I laughed too, out of politeness more than anything else.

Doctor Hoo kept busy. I felt a little bit in the way, to tell you the truth, so I went and had a sit-down on a chair. And while I'm being perfectly honest, I didn't want to see what he was doing. Yes, I know it wasn't a real woman sat sitting there on the table but it still seemed indecent somehow, so I kept my minces averted. It didn't help that she kept talking to me while he was working. Now, if she'd been a real patient, he'd have knocked her out with gas or something. Well, I would hope so, anyway.

"It ain't half exciting!" Sprite enthused. She really was like the child she'd been pretending to be for Gawd knows how many years. But then she brought herself up sharpish and said it was also the most serious thing we could ever be involved with in our lives. She meant ridding London of Foggy Jack once and for all, of course. "Perhaps, when he's gone," she sounded more reflective, "it will be an end to it."

"End to what?" I arsked.

"An end to all this horror and violence. Against women. You might have noticed all his victims have been women? Well, they have. And it was always like that, all along the line. Now, why do you think that is?"

"I don't know… Here, didn't you say something about him thriving on fear? Perhaps women is easier to frighten – is that it?"

"Not at all! If anything, women are much braver than men. Could a man tolerate the pain and responsibility of bearing a child? Not for a bleedin' second, mate. No; you see, Foggy Jack – well, there's more to him than that. He's doing all the blokes a favour, ain't he? He's helping them to keep things the way they are and have always been, ain't he? By demonstrating male dominance over the female. Don't you get it?"

Well, the look on my boat probably told her I didn't. I didn't get it. "All I know is, he's killing birds so he's got to be stopped. Why ain't that enough?"

Even without lungs, Sprite somehow managed to let out a sigh. I decided a change of subject was called for so I made an observation about the weather.

"Nice day for it," I said, jerking my head toward the window – even though the curtains was drawn.

"Let's hope it fogs up a bit later," said Sprite. "The coppers'll need the fog on their side, won't they? To help with their illusion!"

Her voice had taken on that tone that suggested she was talking to an idiot and that idiot was Yours Truly. Well, I didn't have to stand for that – or even sit there. I did stand, actually, but it was only to arsk the doctor whether he wanted anything fetching. I was keen to go out on an errand. I felt like a bit of a spare part, to be honest – and not even one of them spare parts Doctor Hoo would find a use for.

He stopped whatever he was doing and pointed at the ceiling. I thought for a second he was telling me to go and hang myself but then I remembered the room upstairs.

"What?" I had to arsk. "What do you want me to fetch?"

He pointed again, more emphatically this time. I got it; he was sending me upstairs to get me out of the way. Charming!

Well, I wasn't going to stay where I wasn't wanted and to be spoken to like I was not the full shilling, so orf up the stairs I trudged like a kid sent to his room without no supper. I reached the door before I remembered that it would be locked and I'd have to go back down again and arsk for the key, and then I would feel like a garden tool. But I tried the door and it weren't locked, which was odd but I wasn't complaining, so I went into that empty room, only it weren't empty. There was a table with candles on it, and they was lit and showed me a book, that big book like a scrapbook what Hoo had locked in the bureau. There was a chair, pulled out from under the table just a little bit. Like an invitation, I couldn't help thinking.

I'd been sent up there to have a sit-down and a squint at the scrapbook. It was Hoo's way of keeping me out of his way, I suppose. But when I sat down and saw what was in the book, I realised it was more than a keep-Damien-busy exercise. Doctor Hoo wanted me to read it; he wanted me to know.

Funny old sod. He couldn't just tell me himself, could he?

***

My friend – I call you my friend even though at the time of writing, we have yet to meet. You have yet to be born, no doubt; for some reason I see you as much younger than I, but then again, most people are! It is not unheard of for a man to live to be a hundred years old but here I am and, you can attest I am sure, that age has not wearied me nor rendered me weak in wind and limb. It must be said, though, that I am not the man I used to be.

There will come a time when you need to know all of this and so I set it down for you to read. If you cannot read, I shall teach you.

I was Montgomery Hood; you may be aware of this already. My father was a clockmaker and I was his apprentice but all my life I had a passion to help people, to make their lives better, beyond improving their punctuality. I wanted to heal the lame and (this is what landed me in hot water) to prolong life. Indefinitely.

My colleagues in the medical profession were simply not ready for my innovations. Why should a man lose a limb, an organ, or a faculty to illness or accident? Let him have a replacement, I said, and not merely a cosmetic substitute such as a wooden leg or a glass eye. Let him have a fully working new one. Let it be better than the original!

My work was met with scorn and derision. It could not be done, I was told repeatedly. There were naysayers who averred the impossibility of my proposal on technological grounds. The machinery does not exist, they said; our knowledge is not sufficiently advanced. Others raised objections on what they called philosophical or moral grounds – the profession remains plagued and beleaguered by self-righteous short-sightedness to this day. If it is a man's lot to lose a leg, a hand, an eye or what-have-you, then so be it. We may alleviate his discomfort but it is not our place to go against the will of God or, to imitate the Creator by fashioning bits and pieces whenever we feel like it.

There are words for this kind of person but I will not sully your eyes by recording them here.

I was forced to conduct my research in secrecy. I was not alone in this, of course, for many were availing themselves of the services of body-snatchers at the time. My aim was not to reanimate the dead but to improve matters for the living. A dead man's hand attached to the stump of a living man's arm – who could object to that?

At first, I encountered problems with tissue rejection but then I remembered my training at my father's elbow. The human body has its cycles and patterns just as a clock does. I developed increasingly intricate workings to marry dead flesh with living.

Somehow word got out and I was hounded from my Harley Street practice. Those fools! Those blind fools! I vowed to make them see the worth of my endeavours.

At the Lord Mayor's dinner that year, I finagled my way in among the entertainers. I had a very different floor show in mind. The dancers were all patients of mine with new legs and feet. The juggler's hands were my best work. My assembled colleagues (I mean, my fellow professionals gathered rather than put together!) laughed and clapped along but when I revealed myself, the tide turned.

"Heretic!" they called me.

"Abominations!" they deemed my artistes.

They hurled things at us. Food and wine glasses. Flatware and crockery. And then someone lobbed a lantern at my feet.

The conflagration was instantaneous, assisted by the flammable nature of my minstrel garb. I was engulfed by fire. I flailed and thrashed around, unable to breathe, while all around me, people fled in panic. At last, my artistes came to my rescue. One threw water over me. Others yanked the tablecloth free and wrapped me in it, rolling me over and over until the flames were doused. They carried me from the building and back to Harley Street. Through my excruciating pain I managed to signal my wishes. They were to leave me. They were to go out and let it be known that Montgomery Hood was dead.

Which, of course, was a falsehood.

But I was no longer that man. Part of him was gone forever.

Years I spent in solitude, holed up on Harley Street, a physician healing himself, rebuilding and also refining my techniques. I developed a skin-like covering from the rubber plants I kept in my office. As you will have no doubt observed, it has a yellowish quality, lending me a somewhat Oriental appearance. That suited my purposes well, for I did not want anyone to recognise that Hood had survived.

When at last I emerged into daylight, I saw that the exterior of the building had been defaced by my detractors. A coat of paint and a vigorous window-cleaning soon put that to rights but the brass plaque that bore my name had been vandalised as though someone had tried to scratch me from existence. They did not get far – perhaps they were interrupted – and so my name lost its D and I became Hoo.

My enemies aged and died, as men are wont to do but I, with my latex coating did not. As parts of me succumbed to the ravages of time, I replaced them until very little of my original body remains.

(And this last bit was written in darker ink, as though it had been added more recently)

And now, I come to the purpose behind these revelations: I fear our adversary will prove unassailable. I fear he will prevail. I have been aware of his presence in this city for many years, since long before the recent spate of murders. He is there at every accident, at every kind of woe that betides mankind. It is my opinion that he will seek to possess my body, because it is, as far as I can judge, immortal, and will give him the shell he needs in order to travel the world.

YOU MUST NOT LET THIS COME TO PASS.

Here is the key – the key to my heart, no less. Lose it! Destroy it! Then, if the fiend does take possession of my earthly remains it will not last him long.

Perform this final office for me, I beg you, my most loyal and trusted friend.

***

"The key to his heart" – what did that mean? I've always thought the key to my heart was a couple of drinks and a slap-up dinner.

I pocketed the object in question. Perhaps it unlocked a vault or a strongbox containing the secrets of Doctor Hoo's life's work. Although, as I felt the weight of it settle in my jacket, I know that wasn't it. This was the key to much, much more.

Thirty-Two

"You really don't have to do this, Adams," Kipper addressed the sergeant, who looked more than a little put out.

"Might as well, sir, since I've gone to all this trouble." He gestured at his disguise, every detail of which was perfect from the hairpins in his wig to the buckles on his boots.

"I miss your beard," Kipper sighed.

"I don't, sir," Adams was cheerful. "Awful, itchy thing, sir, and hardly hygienic. Turns out I was hiding behind it, sir. I've no need to hide myself away no more."

"Well, I wish you would," said Kipper. "What I mean is, I don't like the idea of you being out there, putting yourself in harm's way. I don't want to lose you, Adams."

"I'm touched, sir." Adams dabbed at his eye with a handkerchief of black lace. "But ain't you worried about them magicians and all, sir, what's putting themselves in harm's way too, sir?"

Kipper grunted. "Those men are professional illusionists, well-practiced in their skills. You ain't."

"I'm going to give it a bloody good go, sir."

"Yes, Adams; I know you will."

***

The time came. The magicians, in their dollymop disguises, stationed themselves at their appointed places as the sun went down. Nervous tension was running high; they were each to give the performance of their lives – and those lives depended on it. One break in the chain would mean the failure of the entire plan. Kipper tapped his feet on the floor of the carriage that was conveying him to Golders Green. He toyed with the handcuffs in his coat pocket. The weight of them was comforting even though he was not expecting to make any arrest that night – for how can one arrest fog?

Panic seized him. There was too much out of his control, too much that could go tits-up. As well as putting the lives of all those men on the line, his entire career was in jeopardy. Was it too late? Was there still time to turn the cab around and get to Whitechapel? He could dismiss the first magician and that would be an end to it.

Except it wouldn't.

Foggy Jack would still be at large and more women would die. And, if Sprite's fears were justified, Foggy Jack would no longer be content with sticking to his patch. He would want to roam the whole world over and many more would die.

It was bonkers. Insane!

Bigby would – Bigby would what? Laugh in Kipper's face and report him? Have him banged up in the loony bin?

He had the cab drop him at the Old Bull and Bush. If I have been followed, he reasoned, it will look like I've come for a quick pint. Followed by whom? That was the sticking point. Who and what was Foggy Jack? What could he see? How much did he know? Was he present in every curl of mist, every drop of airborne condensation? Was he all fog or just made of it, like I am a man but not all mankind?

I'll drive myself around the bloody twist thinking like this! Kipper shook his head as though to dislodge his thoughts.

We will carry on as if our quarry is an individual, a being with limitations. If he's anything else, well, we're fucked.

He turned away from the pub with the invitingly warm gleam at its windows and piano music underscoring the hubbub and general conviviality. Perhaps later – when it was all over – perhaps then there would be time for a pint. He walked the rest of the way – less than a quarter of the mile – to the chosen spot.

Between Golders Green and Hampstead Heath, excavations had begun for an extension to the underground railway. Two hundred feet below the ground – that should do it, Kipper reckoned. That should be deep enough to bury the bastard.

The lure was Coppélia. Doctor Hoo should have her installed by now. Far below Kipper's feet. It had to be down there because if Foggy Jack took possession of the automaton elsewhere in the open, there would be no stopping him. He'd leg it and be orf on his round-the-world killing spree before you could say Jack bleedin' Robinson.

The endgame was to get him underground, lure him to Coppélia – that was Sergeant Adams's part – let him take up occupancy, so to speak, before he realised his new body was welded to the floor. Then it would be a simple matter of filling in the hole and Bob's your auntie's husband.

And then, of course, Kipper would have to persuade the powers that be to abandon the proposed extension.

"Toads!" Sergeant Adams had cried when the subject had come up.

"Couldn't agree more," Kipper had muttered. "Bunch of pen pushers."

"No, sir, I mean toads. As in rare and endangered species, sir. We put it about that the site, being so close to the heath and all, is their natural habitat. There'd be a public outcry if they was wiped out, sir."

"Really?" Kipper's eyebrows had gone skywards. "And how'd you know all this then, eh?"

"Well, sir, in me spare time, sir, I am something of a naturalist."

"Good gawd! That's the last thing we need. I'm only just getting used to seeing you parade around in women's clothing, never mind no clobber at all."

"Ah, no, sir, you see, that's a common mistake. Your naturalist—"

But Kipper had given up listening. The guff about rare toads would be enough to delay the work until he could come up with a better reason. The truth was out of the question.

191

There remained the minor detail of trapping the foggy bastard. All Kipper could do was wait. And try to imagine how each link in the dollymop chain was making his contribution.

Had it already begun, he wondered? Or was the first link – Startling Boffo, or whatever his name was – still waiting on his corner in Whitechapel? Would Foggy Jack even take the bait? With genuine dollymops warned off, there would be slim pickings for him otherwise.

Kipper ran through the chain in his mind from Startling Boffo in Whitechapel to his own Sergeant Adams on the heath. After Startling Boffo came Fontini who would entice Foggy Jack to Old Street, where El Astro would lead him along Islington High Street, and Flash Fingers Freddie would take him from Liverpool Road to Camden Park, where Stroganov the Great would take over in Kentish Town and get the killer to Highgate Road, where Amazo the Amazing's job would be to get him onto Hampstead Heath for Sergeant Adams to take over…

Adams would lead the killer from the heath to the site of the proposed new station where Coppélia would be waiting…

If it doesn't work… Kipper shook his head, allowing no negativity to cloud his thinking. It must work! There was no alternative.

The fog was thickening but out here, away from the city, it was cleaner. Benevolent, you might say, snuggling the scene in a fluffy blanket, shielding the eye from the hands that would suffocate you… Kipper shuddered. The weather made it more likely that Foggy Jack would be on the prowl but it also made it bloody impossible to see what was happening.

He stamped his feet to dispel the chill that was running through his body. Come on, he urged the misty murk. It probably won't be, but it feels like the waiting is the worst part.

And then, a dark shape loomed ahead. Kipper squinted at it as the shape grew larger. It was heading directly toward him, breathing heavily.

Human then, Kipper was relieved to realise. The approaching figure took on definition. Colours appeared and became vivid splashes.

"Oh, sir!" Sergeant Adams cried between gulps of air. "We're done for! It's all gone tits-up, sir!"

Kipper grabbed the sergeant by his shoulders; his shawl was damp with foggy dew. He searched the man's eyes. "What happened?" He tried to keep his voice steady but his heart was galloping as fast as his subordinate's.

Adams shook his head. He took an agonising look over his shoulder and let out a yelp of fear and anguish.

"He's coming, sir! Foggy Jack! He's here!"

Adams collapsed in a faint against the inspector. Kipper struggled to keep upright, shifting the sergeant's weight against his chest. He strained to see over Adams's shoulder, beyond the black cloud of his dislocated wig.

The shape of a man in top hat and opera cloak materialised from the mist and stepped calmly toward the policemen.

"Good evening," he said.

Kipper gasped.

It was Edward, Lord Beighton.

Thirty-Three

The doctor and me carried Coppélia down the shaft what had been dug out for a new tube station or something. He had rebuilt her, restored her to her former glory, only she was better and all. There was the light of life in her eyes on account of that Sprite creature being in residence inside her. Sprite had tried to insist she could walk it, make her own way to the underground cavern but Doctor Hoo wasn't having none of it. We put her in a crate to keep her hidden from prying eyes, because you never know who might be about – especially up near Hampstead Heath way.

She weren't half heavy and we nearly dropped her a couple of times and I thought my old Union Jack ain't going to thank me for this in the morning – if I get to the morning, that is. We might all be dead by then and then a bad back would be the least of my worries.

And so, down in the tube station at midnight, we jemmied the front off of the crate and Sprite did her best to arrange Coppélia in her best come-and-get-it pose. The idea was, when Foggy Jack come down and saw her, he'd step into the crate and me and the doctor would spring out from behind it and nail it shut. Then we'd scarper out of there pretty sharpish. As soon as we come out on top, a team of navvies would fill up the shaft with all the dirt they'd dug out of it. Only at this point, the navvies hadn't bleedin' turned up. Still in the pub, I reckoned. Still down at the Old Bull and Bush. I told Doctor Hoo he shouldn't have bleedin' paid them before they'd done the job. So it looks like it'll be me and old Inspector Fishface getting busy with the shovels when the time comes. Thank you very much.

When I addressed this matter to the doctor, I wasn't sure he was taking it all in. Here, Doctor, I says, are you all right? Only he don't answer. You ain't half looking run down, I says, only because it's true. You want to look after yourself. And his lip sort of gives a twitch like he's trying to smile at me only he decides it's too much like hard work.

So, with Coppélia in place, I had to chivvy him along. "Come on; what's the matter with you? Get your arse behind the crate so he don't see you."

I've never seen him so dozy. I bundled him behind the box and I had just enough time to get myself squirreled away before we heard commotion from up top. It was all kicking off up there. My heart was thumping; this is it!

And then we heard something what put a stop to all the shouting all of a sudden.

Gunshots!

Two of 'em.

Thirty-Four

"Stay back!" Kipper cried. A dark thought flashed across his mind: Sergeant Adams would serve as a shield if Beighton came at him with a blade. No. That was wrong. He set the sleeping policeman carefully on the ground and stood tall to face his foe.

"Steady on," said Lord Beighton. "It's not what you think. Honestly."

He held out his hands to show they were empty.

"How did you get out of the nick?" Kipper's eyes narrowed with suspicion.

"Ah, it's the queerest thing," said Beighton. "There I was, in my cell, feeling all sorts of sorry for myself when it began to get cold in there. And unpleasant. Colder and more unpleasant than it already was, I mean – Let's face it, it's hardly the Dorchester. I saw mist coiling through the keyhole and forming a cloud. That cloud took on the shape of a man. I have never been more terrified in all my days, let me tell you."

"Foggy Jack!" Kipper gasped.

"We were not formally introduced but yes, I suppose it was." Beighton shuddered at the memory. "He laughed and said, in a deep and horrible voice, that he could help me. He could get me out of my current predicament in seconds flat, and I said something about there was no way I could get out the way he had come in – the things one thinks of in moments of duress! – and he laughed again and said all I had to do was let him in. Let him inside me and let him do the rest. Well, I told him I was not that way inclined, despite what went on at boarding school, and he laughed again and assured me it was nothing of that sort. I asked what was the catch and he told me I was a very astute gentleman and no mistake. Lead me to Kipper, he said. And I said I don't know where he is. And he said you could find out. And I said I couldn't see how, being stuck in this hole, and he said you haven't been listening; I can get you out. He was losing patience with me, I could tell – lucky he didn't have my throat out on the spot.

"Well, what option did I have? Certain he would kill me if I denied him, I agreed to his terms. What would you have done, Inspector? What would anyone have done? I sat on my bunk and closed my eyes. It was a curious sensation. Akin to sitting in a draught and then becoming the draught, if you see what I mean. I opened my eyes and nothing had changed, except the foggy man wasn't there.

"Oh, I'm here all right – his voice was in my head, like the pinch of a hangover the morning after a night on the tiles, what! Relax, he said, like that was even an option. Allow me to take the reins."

"I got to my feet – or rather, he got to my feet. Another curious sensation: like when you're blind blotto and yet somehow you manage to walk. I – he – We moved to the door and he made my hands reach for the buttons on my trousers. He cursed, which was excruciating, and I said, Let me do it. I unfastened my trousers and let them drop to my ankles. Before I could give voice to a question about this turn of events, he has my old chap working. Nice handiwork, he observed, extending the brass thing and setting it spinning."

"You drilled your way out," said Kipper, flatly. "Like you did with that prostitute."

Beighton reddened. "I tell you, that was not my fault. I am just as much a victim as that poor woman."

"Tell that to the beak," said Kipper. "How did you get up here? How did you know where to find me?"

"I merely asked the man at the front desk. He looked me up and down and asked, bizarrely, if I was one of the inspector's magicians. Foggy Jack answered for me. Yes, he said. After that, the man, a constable, I suppose he was, spilled the beans. He told us you would be here so here we headed, and now here we are."

"We?" Kipper glanced around. "You seem your old self again. Where is he?"

"I'm awfully sorry, Inspector," Lord Beighton stepped back. Kipper became aware of someone standing behind him. He turned around.

"Inspector!" said Foggy Jack. "How delightful to see you!"

Kipper paled. The body of Sergeant Adams lurched toward him, against the will of the original owner, it seemed. Adams's eyes rolled and his head shook, helpless to prevent the advances of the evil spirit within him.

"Stay back!" Kipper yelled. "Get out of my sergeant!" he commanded.

Other voices and police whistles sounded as Bigby and his team from Scotland Yard appeared from the fogbound heath.

"I say! Stop where you are!" Bigby cried. His police-issue pistol was aimed squarely at the sergeant's chest.

"No!" cried Kipper. "Don't shoot him! Adams, fight it! Stand still, man!"

"Trying…to…sir…" Adams grunted, but his feet slid forward, edging closer to the inspector.

Bigby shot him. Twice.

Sergeant Adams fell to the ground.

Thirty-Five

I was out of that shaft like a rat up a drainpipe. Well, down there we was sitting ducks, wasn't we? Out in the open I'd have more of a chance of getting away. I nipped behind a stack of building materials – wood for propping up the tunnels, I suppose; I didn't really have the time to take an inventory – and I was horrified by the scene playing out in front of me. The sergeant who seemed to like wearing women's clobber was lying on the ground. I could see it was him on account of his wig being orf and his ginger hair glowing in the mist. He wasn't moving. As for Fishface, he was standing there with his hands in the air, like he was being held up or something. That bloke from Scotland Yard was pointing a gun at him and at that bleedin' toff – how did *he* get here? – and he was screaming.

"Which one? Which one of you is it?"

"Ain't me," said Kipper.

"Not I," said the toff. "I can assure you."

"If you shoot us, it won't make no difference."

That Bigby bloke scowled. "Do you mean it won't make a difference or it will make a difference? Honestly, old man, your propensity to speak in double negatives can prove perplexing."

"Do what?" said Kipper.

"But if I shoot you both, that's two less places for him to hide, no?"

"No!" cried Kipper and the toff in alarm.

I came out of my hiding place. "Here, you'll have to shoot me and all," I said with my hands in the air so he could see them. "And all your blokes and all. And yourself, come to think of it."

"He's right," said the toff.

Bigby was dithering. "All right!" he capitulated. He lowered his gun and that was when Foggy Jack made his move. Via the physical form of Edward, Lord Beighton. He shoved the inspector into Bigby and lurched toward me, with his more recent leg leading the way. I sprang back but it wasn't me he was after. He gave me a laugh of contempt as he went by, on his way to the shaft. Foggy Jack was going underground.

"You fool!" said Kipper. "You've led him straight to it."

"Hang on," I stood up for myself. "Wasn't that the bleedin' plan?"

"Well… yes. But you were supposed to be down there and all, you berk."

"Oh, yeah," I said.

We – Kipper, Bigby, and me – hurried to the mouth of the shaft. Bigby had his gun poised again, as if that was going to bleedin' help. Coppers with guns – I'm against that kind of thing.

"It's awfully quiet down there," Bigby observed.

"It'd be bleedin' quiet up here and all," snapped Kipper, "if you shut your bleedin' trap."

"Ladies, please! A bit of hush!" I raised my voice. Shouting at coppers – I'm all in favour of that.

It did the trick. We all shut our traps and listened, bent over that hole like we was contemplating chucking ourselves into it. Bigby was right: it was quiet. Too quiet.

Long minutes dragged by. What the hell was going on down there?

"I'm going down," I said, almost out of my mind with the not-knowing. The coppers grabbed my arms and pulled me back. And I wondered if I could somehow unfasten my arms, the arms what the doctor had given me, and escape. Mind you, if I did, I wouldn't be much use with no chalk farms, would I? Well, I could still kick somebody's arse, I suppose.

A slam! From the underground chamber, followed by a slow clink-clink-clink.

"Somebody's climbing up!" I whispered.

We peered over the edge. Bigby's gun was shaking so much if it had been a bleedin' barn climbing up that ladder, he wouldn't have hit it.

"Who is it?" said Kipper, as if we knew the bleedin' answer.

"Ssh!" hissed Bigby. "I'm trying to focus."

We watched and we waited as a shape emerged from the depths. A patch of yellow, like dim candlelight, grew as it rose toward us.

Coppélia's blonde wig.

"Here," said Sprite from inside the decoy dollymop, "You gents going to give me a hand or what?"

Kipper and me heaved our shoulders in relief but Bigby weren't so happy to see the rubber-faced tart. He kept his gun trained on her.

"How do we know it's not...him?" he jabbered but me and Kipper ignored him and we helped her out of the hole.

"This is Sprite," said Kipper. "Sprite, this is Bigby of the Yard."

"Yard?" laughed Sprite, looking Bigby pointedly in the crotch. "I'd say three inches at the most."

"What happened down there, girl?" I arsked. "Why have you come out?"

Her shoulders clunked as she shrugged them. "I think I became surplus to requirements, on account of Foggy Jack finding a different host."

Bigby was incandescent. "What in blue blazes is going on?" He may even have stamped his foot. "What is this – thing?" He pointed his pipe at Coppélia, who didn't look too impressed with him neither.

"Later," said Kipper. He rounded on Sprite. "Tell us what happened and sharpish!"

"All right; keep your hair on. Well, that toff come down, didn't he? I don't know what we was expecting but it weren't him, only he's having a bit of trouble, like he's trying to come down and go back up at the same time. Help me, he says in a posh voice, I can't hold him orf indefinitely. And me and Doctor Hoo glances at each other and it's like we both understands: Foggy Jack can't completely control a human body. Not for long. That's why he ain't run orf with one before now and gorn orf around the world. And this toff, he's putting up a good fight. And the doctor and me looks at each other again and there's that understanding between us, and we grabs the toff by his arms and flings him into the crate. Foggy Jack roars in surprise and we shoves the front on the crate and I hammers it on – I'm stronger and faster and can use me fist instead of a hammer. Besides, the doctor ain't looking too clever. He's sluggish, looks exhausted. Like a clock struggling from tick to tock. And I says we'd better shift ourselves and he waves me away – he can barely lift his arm. Well, Foggy Jack is pounding on the inside of the crate – or maybe it's the toff, not too keen on the idea of being buried alive. And the doctor sinks to the ground and it's like the crate is going to burst open, so I gets out of there and, well, here I am."

She grabbed Kipper's arm – tight it must have been because I saw him wince. "Protect me, Inspector! I don't want Foggy Jack coming after me."

"Is that likely?" said Kipper, only I ain't sure who he was arsking.

"I'd say," said Sprite. "This body's a bleedin' marvel. Indestructible, I shouldn't wonder. I'd like to hang on to it."

"But what about the doctor?" I peered into the shaft. "Won't Foggy Jack get inside him?"

"I shouldn't think so," said Sprite. She put a hand on my shoulder – it was quite a wallop; she don't know her own strength. "He's… *stopped*, love. That's the only word for it."

And I felt the weight of the key he had given me. The key to his heart. And I understood.

There came a roar and a rush of air and a great cloud of fog poured up from the shaft and formed the shape of a man in the sky.

"Fools!" Foggy Jack grumbled like thunder. "No wooden box can hold me."

He threw something at our feet, something red and pink and yellow. It was the head of Edward, Lord Beighton. Bigby fired his gun at the demon in the sky until he ran out of bullets. Foggy Jack laughed, sending a shiver down our spines. It was the sound of pure evil.

"Very well, gentlemen," his voice rumbled, like thunder as I said, like an underground train but in the sky. "I shall cease butchering your womenfolk. For now. They have served their purpose in bringing the esteemed doctor out of the woodwork. He's the one I'm after, except he doesn't seem to be as lively as he once was."

"Fuck off," sneered Inspector Fishface, surprising us all. "You're finished in this town. We're on to you. You'll never be corporeal."

"Big word, Johnny," I heard that Bigby mutter. "I'm impressed."

And then Foggy Jack's eyes glowed red and fixed on me and his face twisted into a malevolent grin. It was like I was glued to the spot.

"I see you," he said. "I will find you."

With that, he disappeared, dissolving along with the rest of the mist as the first streaks of sunrise broke up the darkness with pink and gold. His minces was the last to go, like he was the bleedin' Cheshire Cat of supernatural murderers or something.

"Lucky for you the sun come up, I reckon," said Sprite.

But I didn't feel lucky at all. Not by a long chalk.

"I don't understand," said Kipper. "Why didn't he come after Coppélia when he had the chance?"

"I'd like to have seen him try," said Sprite, holding up Coppélia's fists like a prize-fighter about to spar. "I've become rather attached to this body, even if it is a false one."

"I know," I said, my hand closing around the key in my pocket. "He's got his eyes on a bigger prize."

Thirty-Six

What a mess. What a bloody mess. Inspector Kipper tried to make sense of the night's events. Sergeant Adams was alive – that was the main thing. He would spend a long time recuperating in hospital but he would recover. Whether he would come back to work or not was yet to be determined. Knowing Adams, Kipper reflected, wild horses wouldn't keep him away from Bow Street nick.

Perhaps it was a good thing that the macabre Doctor Hoo was out of commission and Sergeant Adams would have to go without new parts. Kipper shivered; the world's not ready for that kind of medicine.

"Lovely to see you, sir!" Adams tried to sit up in bed when Kipper came in. "Them's nice blooms."

Kipper placed the bunch of flowers on a bedside table. "You're looking better than last time I saw you."

"Bless you, sir. Did you catch him?"

Kipper reddened. "Not exactly. But don't you worry about that. You just worry about getting back on your pins."

Adams nodded at a chair in the corner of the room. Kipper brought it to his bedside and perched on it. "I'd make you a cuppa but I ain't best disposed to at the minute, sir."

"That's all right."

The pair sat in companionable silence. Kipper wondered whether he should tell the sergeant how relieved he was, how worried he had been. But, he found he didn't have to utter a word. Adams, as ever, seemed to know what the inspector was going to say before Kipper knew himself.

"I've been thinking, sir," Adams looked away. "Get a lot of time to do that, lying here. Thinking about things. Life is short, sir, and mine was very nearly all the shorter. So I'm sorry but I ain't coming back to work, sir. Not as a copper."

Kipper's jaw dropped. "Don't be so – I mean, I shall – the force will miss you, man."

"You're very kind, sir. But I'm going to try a new career, ain't I? I've been thinking about it ever since I first put on women's clothes."

Kipper was aghast. "Don't tell me you're going to be a dollymop!"

Adams chuckled, so much his injuries pinched him. "No, sir, Lord above, no sir. Soon as I've got me strength back, I'm orf down the music hall, sir. See if I can't get me a job as a female impersonator. Sort of like Dan Leno, sir. Them magicians – who still want paying for that engagement, sir – they said they'll help me out. Sorry to leave you to muddle along without me. You look like you don't know what to say, sir."

"No, no," Kipper reached for his former sergeant's hand and gave it a squeeze. "What I want to say, Ben, is you don't have to be sorry."

***

"Back again, love?" cackled the flower-seller on the Portobello Road. "Twice in one day, I am honoured."

Kipper grunted and paid for his second bunch of flowers. The first was standing gaily in a vase beside Adams's hospital bed. This second he would take home…

Bigby had taken control. Again, perhaps that was a good thing. "Beighton killed one woman; this much we know," he'd said, pacing outside the shaft and puffing on his pipe. "He knew we were on to him, so he has absconded. Left the country, I shouldn't wonder. He won't trouble the streets of London again."

"A cover-up?" Kipper had been surprised.

"Literally," said Bigby. He signalled to his men who set about filling in the shaft.

"I don't like it," said Kipper with a petulant expression.

"You would rather report the truth, old man? They'll whisk you orf to Bedlam as soon as look at you."

Bigby had been right. Kipper could see that and was willing to live with it. And if it should all go belly-up, Bigby as the presiding officer would cop the shit storm. Not that any of it should ever come to light. The railway people were abandoning their proposed extension; too expensive. Too much negative publicity about toads, he shouldn't be surprised.

One thing he had insisted on before the dirt went raining down on the remains of Edward, Lord Beighton: the removal of Doctor Hoo from the underground tomb. The world might not be ready for his brand of medicine but one day it might. Kipper had the doctor transported to a secret location, the details of which he kept sealed in the safe at Bow Street.

While all this was going on, that Deacus fellow had legged it. Can't say I blame him, Kipper thought. Best off out of it. Don't know where he's gone and I don't want to. Going to try to put all this business behind me and get back to nicking pickpockets and chasing burglars. Oh, for the easy life!

He turned the key in the front door and pushed his way through to the communal hallway. Like a tiger in the undergrowth, landlady Mrs Plum sprang from behind an aspidistra.

"There you are, Inspector!" she displayed unerring mental acuity. "Nice to have you home. Spot of dinner suit you? It'll be ready in ten. Oh, ain't they lovely blooms?" She clasped her string of pearls in surprise. "For me, are they? Oh, Inspector Kipper! You shouldn't have!"

"I didn't," said Kipper, heading up the stairs. "No dinner for me, thank you, Mrs Plum. I have other arrangements."

Mrs Plum's eyes widened and she actually staggered backwards. "What's this?" she gasped. "Don't tell me you've been and gone and found yourself a lady friend?"

But Kipper said nothing. He bounded up the stairs, taking them two or three at a time, whistling to himself and holding the bunch of flowers like the Olympic torch.

He knocked the door to his own room before going in. "Only me," he said. He shut the door behind him and held out the flowers.

Coppélia turned from the window and smiled.

Thirty-Seven

I stayed in my cabin the entire journey. Something about being on a steamship made me uneasy. The steam, I suppose. Too much like fog. The spray of water over the decks, too much like mist. And I must keep away from fog and mist.

I'm heading for the desert. This train will take me to California. There's a place there called Death Valley, one of the hottest places on this Earth.

Foggy Jack won't find me there.

That's what I'm hoping, anyway.

Sometimes I think I should have said goodbye. To Doctor Hoo, I mean. I think that stinging feeling behind my eyes is guilt, what I ain't never experienced before. I should have gone down that shaft and said goodbye. Even if it was like talking to a stopped clock, I should have said it. But I didn't; I was too keen on getting away and saving me own bushel and peck. I had no time for hanging about.

Perhaps I'm being overly cautious. Perhaps he's still confined to London. Foggy Jack, I mean. I'd like to believe that so I can sleep at night, but I doubt it. I doubt it very much.

That bastard will have found a way to get out of the city. I saw the way he looked at me. I can see it now, those red eyes glowing like coals, every time I close my eyes. There's no way he's going to let me get away.

He wants the key. He wants the key to Doctor Hoo.

And I'm going to spend the rest of my life, in hiding, like I'm buried alive, making sure he don't get it.

THE END

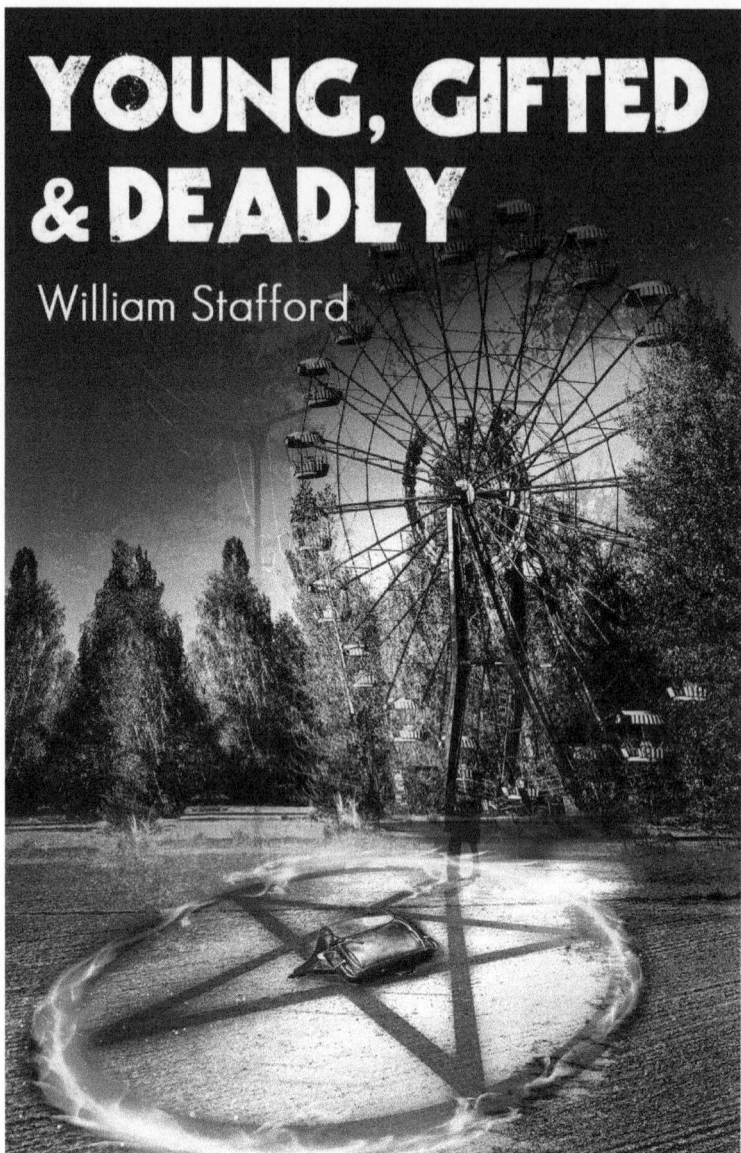

YOUNG, GIFTED & DEADLY

William Stafford

Lightning Source UK Ltd.
Milton Keynes UK
UKHW040631141122
412172UK00001B/210

9 781785 385445